Fall Without Jerry

By

Henri Rosenblum

In Nocte Consilium
Zzzzzzzzzzzzzzzzz

ISBN-13: 978-0692386248 (Sway Publishing)

Fall Without Jerry
is dedicated

to my incredible children,
Keith, Sarah, and Lauren,

to the guy who fell at Red Rocks,

to Adam Katz,

and to Jerry.

contents

acknowledgements

Thanks to the Grateful Dead and the entire Grateful Dead extended family for so many happy years and good times.

Thanks to Robert Hunter for your lyrics. They are enlightening, inspirational, and paint beautiful images.

Thanks to Mick and Keith for Sway

Thanks to Ted Smits and Alyssa Trumper at TED-TV for their PDF wizardry.

Thanks to my family and friends.

Thanks to all the characters that appear in this story, real and imaginary, and somewhere in between.

aox

Words by Robert Hunter
Ramble On Rose
The Eleven
Wharf Rat
Box Of Rain
Terrapin Station
Attics Of My Life
The Wheel
That's It For The Other One
Stella Blue
Truckin'
Ripple

Words by Jerry Garcia
Cryptical Envelopment

Words by Bob Weir
The Faster We Go The Rounder We Get

aoxo

1 home for the holidays

The autumn leaves were on fire, a kaleidoscope of reds, yellows, and oranges hanging precariously in the trees. Every so often one would set itself free, float earthward, and kindly settle atop a sea of green grass. Nature, ever changing, in all her glory, running through my mind's eye like a perfect dose of shrooms, or a hit of crystal blue.

I was looking through the front bay window at the Nyack home of my Uncle Lou and Aunt Estelle. The occasion was Rosh Hashanah dinner. My chubby cousin Trudi was there with her new skinny boyfriend, and my cousin Henry was being ribbed/tormented by my Uncle Teddy about getting the mop for a drink that had spilled back in 1964. Aunt Estelle, Aunt Ginny, my mother, and my sister Sheila were minding the pots in the kitchen. My father was on the phone with one of his bookies. It was my first time attending holiday dinner in too many years to count.

My fiancée, Alexandra, was home in Manhattan at her apartment on Central Park West nursing a migraine. Earlier that day when I half-heartedly suggested that she accompany me to celebrate Rush-a Homa with my relatives, that some chicken soup might be good for her headache, she responded in perfect Great Neck nasal drone, "Just tell them that my head is exploding."

Somehow the idea of her head exploding seemed okay. And maybe getting engaged to Alexandra this past spring wasn't such a great idea. I loved her, I guess, and socially and financially it was a no-brainer, after all she was a Scoopneck of the renowned New York Scoopnecks, but she wasn't my soul mate, and I knew it. Lately the thought of spending the rest of my life with her was making my ass itch, and not just a little bit, but a whole lot.

An easy wind caused the leaves on the lawn to cartwheel and pirouette, reminding me of these two beautiful girls I had observed spinning endlessly at a Grateful Dead concert that I scammed my way into at the Red Rocks Amphitheatre in Colorado back in 1979. With red soot covering their bare feet up to the silver bangles on their ankles, and free flowing lavender and tangerine peasant dresses topped off with loose fitting halter tops, these long haired blonde visions of loveliness had spun their carefree cosmic dance into my permanent memory. I recalled the magnificence of the starlit sky hovering above; the Dead bouncing music off the colossal red rocks, electricity running through the crowd, and the girls went round and round and round, and the girls went round and round. I inhaled deeply, imagining vividly that I was breathing clean Colorado air. I wished I had been bold enough to strike up a conversation with the younger of the two dancing angels, but at the time I was an awkward seventeen year-old with hardly a whisker on my chin, or a dollar to my name.

A dazzling golden leaf tumbled through the air leaving behind a trail of gold dust, and all it had ever known, to embark on a journey en route for Aoxomoxoa. I pressed my nose against the chilly pane and grasped the sill for support as my knees lightly buckled beneath me. I yearned to be an autumn leaf on a journey. Free to travel, any way the wind blows.

I envied nature; because my seemingly fulfilling life was anything but natural, nor, as of late, fulfilling. My dream job working as a high powered attorney in New York City had become an incessant grind of twelve hour days. My expensive suits felt like prison garb. Even my Jerry Garcia ties choked the air that I so desperately needed to breathe. And my plastic relationship with concrete Alexandra was weighing me down, down, down. For a little over a month I had been teetering on the edge of uncertainty. Nature could change. Why couldn't I? And if I could change, how would I begin?

A strong gust exploded the tranquil autumn scene into frenzy. Leaves flew to and fro, bombarding my field of vision, derailing my reality, spinning, spinning, cascading, sending wave after vibratory wave rolling up my spine, overwhelming my cranium incredibly, magically generating a tangible audible soundtrack to accompany the delusion.

**I'm gonna sing you
a hundred verses in ragtime**

"So Matthew," asked Uncle Lou as he handed me a glass of Manischewitz, "after all these years, you honor us with your presence at holiday dinner. And to what do we owe such an honor?"

And now, transfixed in a purple haze, acting funny, I was oblivious to my uncle's banter, submerged in the distant memory of lost chances with sweet soul sisters, yearning to kiss the sky, the starlit Colorado sky, or any sky for that matter, other than the telltale red pink sky of this past August 9th that had symbolically hung over my head for the past several weeks, nudging me blindly forward, leaving me lost yet without desolation, possessing a resolute feeling that I was fine. But was I?

**I know this song it ain't
never gonna end.**

"Matthew, Matthew can you hear me," repeated my Uncle?

**I'm gonna march you
up and down
the local county line
Take you to the leader
of the band**

"Matthew, answer your uncle," my mother pleaded. She took me by the hand and sat me down on the plastic slipcovered holiday only couch.

"What, oh I'm sorry, was someone talking to me?"

"Yes," said Uncle Lou, "I was saying how nice it is to have you join us for the holidays after all these years."

"Thanks Uncle Lou. It's good to be here." I couldn't have sounded any less sincere. I turned my gaze back toward the window to watch the leaves dance.

"He's not himself, Lou," my mother confided.

"Then who is he?" asked Uncle Lou.

At the time I heard the sad news, I wasn't at all surprised. After all, all things must pass. When you consider the coma, the drug addiction problems, and his ballooning weight; I figured he had been on borrowed time since at least the mid-eighties. As always, I caught the summer shows at The Meadowlands, and had already sent in my mail order for tickets to all six fall-tour performances scheduled at Madison Square Garden. Yet here I was at my Aunt and Uncle's house for holiday dinner. And although I was fully cognizant of my surroundings, I was immersed in a clash of cerebral Ping-Pong between the Jews of Nyack, 5456, and the Dead at Red Rocks, 1979. And the girls went round and round and round, and the girls went round and round.

Goodbye,
Momma and Poppa
Goodbye, Jack and Jill
The grass ain't greener,
the wine ain't sweeter
either side of the hill

"So Matthew, how are things at the firm?"

Asked my Aunt Estelle as she sat next to me on the matching plastic slipcovered recliner. "And where's Alexandra?"

**Did you say
your name was
Ramblin' Rose?
Ramble on, baby
Settle down easy**

"Matthew!", my aunt was now tapping me on the leg.

I slowly raised myself off the couch, played two choppy air guitar chords, and bellowed, "Ramble on Rose."

We all moved to the dinner table to consume the sumptuous feast for thirty that my aunt had prepared for the eleven of us. I apologized to everyone for being so distant, but I couldn't shake my stupor.

After dessert, I drove my BMW325i convertible back to Manhattan listening to a totally smoking '71 Fillmore East bootleg that features Duane Allman playing slide guitar on "Sugar Magnolia", "It Hurts Me Too", and "Beat It On Down The Line". As Duane and Jerry took turns bending notes my mind raced across numerous Grateful Dead shows I had attended at the Garden in falls past. One show in particular, the last of six in September 1993 kept creeping into my conscious. The first set was just seven songs, but it climaxed in an almost hour long "Birdsong". Then "Dark Star" anchored an extraordinary second set that also featured an entirely Philicious "Wharf Rat". That night's performance was, as my best friend and fellow Dead enthusiast Rich Reiner had said for months after the final note had been played, "Amazing, amazing, amazing, amazing, AMAZING!"

Attending Grateful Dead shows meant infinitely more to me than just a concert experience. It represented a collective connection, like the Borg, between myself, the Dead, and everyone else on the scene, simultaneously generating, cultivating, sharing, and imbibing the energy derived from the beautiful music, and the perception that mean people suck.

I had attended indoor shows and outdoor shows, huge festival shows and shows at armpit small-town hockey arenas. I had partied in the nosebleeds, and had also at numerous other shows successfully navigated to the front row to share a second or two of eye contact with Jerry, Phil or Bob, or minutes with Mickey. I had attended as a poor student and as a successful attorney. I had jumped the turnstiles, snuck in with the caterer, forged hand stamps, and bamboozled my way into shows when I couldn't find a ticket, and in prosperous times had given away my extras to 'I Need a Miracle' carefree blonde lovelies in flowing peasant dresses. I had flown to California, driven to Colorado, and hitchhiked to Utica, New York in a blizzard, all to catch shows. At Grateful Dead shows I had watched people live, and on one fateful afternoon at Red Rocks Amphitheater in Colorado, had even watched someone die.

After attending nearly 100 shows over the past twenty years, my cup was not yet full. Even if the tour had gone on forever, I would never be completely satisfied. The realization that there would be no more Grateful Dead shows to attend was an extremely bitter pill to swallow.

The fall tour was cancelled.

Jerry was dead.

2 <u>the eleven eleven</u>

My bedroom phone awoke me from a sound slumber. It was my legal assistant, Lisa. She said, "Hey Matt, late night?"

Groggily I responded, "Uhhh, what time is it?"

"What time is it? It's eight fucking forty-five in the morning boss, and here comes your nine o'clock appointment with the rep from Phillip Morris, truckin' down the hall."

**No more time to tell how
This is the season of what**

"Matt, hello Matt, are you there?"

"Yeah Lisa, I'm here. My nine o'clock, right, stall him."

I fought to free crunchies from the inner corners of my eyes. They clung like sea urchins.

"Don't sweat it big boss man. I'll tell the rep that you're on your way in from the airport and send him to the club for a massage. Just be here by..."

**Eight sided whispering
hallelujah hatrack**

"...over breakfast at Aggies."

"That's fine Lisa, and be certain to assure him that..."

**Now is the time of returning
With thought jewels polished
and gleaming**

"Matt, are you okay?"

**Six proud walkers
on the jingle bell rainbow**

"Just tell the rep that I can't meet with him today. In fact reschedule all my appointments." Click.

**Now is the time past believing
The child has
relinquished the reign**

It felt good to do something ballsy. Actually, it felt great! I hopped out of bed feeling revitalized, and hungry. I opened the fridge, grabbed two eggs, and mindlessly dropped them to the floor. As if in a trance I made oatmeal with raisins. I hadn't eaten oatmeal with raisins in quite some time. It was delicious.

Ring ring ring, ring ring ring...ring ring ring, ring ring ring...ring ring ring, ring ring ring...ring ring ring, ring ring ring...

I let my answering machine pick up, "Hello, thank you for calling 212-555-0681, I'm presently unable to take this call, you know what to do, thanks for tryin' one...Beeeeep."

"Hello Matt... c'mon Matt pick up, I know you're there. Nice joke buddy, but what gives? Matty boy......" Click. It was my immediate boss and friend Roger 'The Rajah' Dalrymple.

I stared blankly at the phone, running my hands through my stylishly coiffed hair, recalling when it used to rest on my shoulders. I took a long swallow of my designer coffee, noting that it tasted of technology. I sat down on the Persian rug in my living room and mindlessly began to gently stretch my back and legs. My muscles were tight and sore. I felt old, and trapped. My carefree youth gone in the blink of a corporate eye. I needed desperately to break free, to feel free, to be free. My brain was churning.

**Five men writing
with fingers of gold**

I dialed my travel agent Benny.

"Hello Benny, Matthew Baron here."

"My man Matthew, zop, let me guess, the eleven to Boston, zip zop, right."

I laughed at the irony. "Well Ben, you got "The Eleven" part right, but Boston, not this time. How about something a bit more exotic?"

"How about Bangkok at eleven eleven?" he joked.

**Now is the test
of the boomerang
Tossed in the night
of redeeming**

My senses were reeling. I felt my big toe shoot up in my slipper. "Done. Put it on my Amex."

"Zippetty zip zip zop, are you sure?"

"Shit sure and ready to tour."

"All right! You go counselor. And what

about the return?"

"Keep it open."

"That's a hefty fare. Zop."

"Fuck it. Book it. Bye." Click.

Whalebelly
Fade away in moonlight
Sink beneath the waters
to the coral sands below

3 <u>khao san road</u>

I arrived the next day at Bangkok International Airport at five fifteen in the evening, Bangkok time. That's right, out of my brain on the five fifteen. Free of baggage, I readily passed through customs and stepped outside the air-conditioned terminal into the sauna that is Southeast Asia in September. I flagged down a taxi.

I crouched in and told the driver, "Khao San Road please."

Khao San Road is a mystical, you need it they got it traveler's safe haven, nestled in downtown Bangkok just a hop, skip, and a jump from the airport. Over the years I had listened as travelers more worldly than I would relive this journey or that adventure, often mentioning a layover at Khao San Road. It was also the only place I knew to go.

The driver answered back, "Okay, Kosahnwode."

The remarkably tiny car pulled away, and BANG, reality check. I was in Thailand!

I shook my head from side to side and muttered to myself, "Thailand, what the fuck am I doing in Thailand? Sure, Jerry's dead, and my fiancée is a bit of a drag, but Thailand.... I must be losing it."

My Levis and white Gap shirt were soaked in sweat. At least I'd had the good sense to wear my Tevas. My only possessions were my passport, my wallet containing 211 dollars and credit cards, my CD Walkman, and 12 compact discs, which fit conveniently into a durable Case Logic case.

The 12 discs were *Skull and Roses* and *American Beauty* - Grateful Dead, *Eat a Peach* - Allman Brothers Band, *Live at Leeds* - The Who, *Magical Mystery Tour* - Beatles, *Sticky Fingers* - Rolling Stones, *Led Zeppelin I*, *Axis: Bold As Love* - Jimi Hendrix, *On The Beach* - Neil Young, *Fear of Music* - Talking Heads, *Legend* - Bob Marley, and Zoot Allures - Frank Zappa.

The cab stopped.

"Kosahnwode."

I handed the driver a twenty.

"No chench po dallah. You go now. Tenk you belly much."

I stepped from the cab into a half-eaten carton of chicken in green curry sauce. Two slant-eyed eight year-olds held their bellies as they laughed, then disappeared into an alley. I grabbed hold of a signpost and shook the slop off my foot and onto the cab's bumper as it pulled away into the hot Bangkok night. Across the street a large tattooed pig snorted at me. I swung a one-eighty, and proceeded directly into the Hello Bar. I scored a beer and sat down at a table. In the dimly lit room sat about twenty people of varying origins, hairstyles, and modes of dress. I thought to myself, incredible, look at all the freaks. In the corner of the dimly lit room, hanging from chains, was a color television. It was showing the film *Conan the Barbarian*, the first one. On screen Conan and his fellow barbarian are sitting by a fire, dining on carcass barbeque.

Conan says, "So... which Gods do you pray to?"

I burst out laughing.

Everyone in the bar looked at me. Then they all returned to watching the film. Someone let out a deep long belch. Everyone raised their right fist and pressed their right thumb to their forehead. They all looked around the room at each other, then at me.

They were also eyeing a couple making out at the bar. The person next to the couple tapped the girl on the shoulder. She opened her eyes, pulled away from the guy she was kissing, and immediately pressed her thumb to her forehead. Seeing the girl triggered the guy to press his thumb to his forehead. Then a girl from the table next to me, a kind of healthy looking Kate Moss doppelganger reached over with her free hand and smacked me firmly on my forehead. Everyone in the room laughed and lowered their hands. They all returned to watching the movie.

Stunned, I asked the girl, "What did you do that for?"

She answered in an Australian accent, "Welcome to Khao San Road mate. Sorry 'bout the blow to the head, but you'll catch on."

I sat listening, rubbing my forehead.

"It's a game that the Swedes play. Last one up after someone burps gets slugged. It's all in good fun. How long have you been travelin' mate?"

"About two days, I just flew in from New York."

"Two days! Well that explains the denims."

"How long have you been traveling?"

"Next week makes two years."

"Two years," I responded a bit in disbelief. "That's a long time to be on the road. Sounds like you're on tour."

"On tour?"

"Never mind."

"No tell me." she insisted.

"Back home the saying goes, shit sure and ready to tour."

"Wait a minute; you're not going to tell me you follow around some band to attend all their concerts..."

"BURRRRRRPPP!!!"

Thumbs started toward foreheads throughout the room. My Aussie acquaintance looked around, placed her thumb to her forehead and again whacked me on my forehead. She said, "Really, you've got to be quicker."

"The Grateful Dead, you were about to say the Grateful Dead."

"Yeah, that's right, the Grateful Dead. A guy I snorkeled with last month on Bali had some cassettes of their music. He said that they were the best. I thought they sounded like a badly beaten Rugby team, getting pissed, howling at the moon."

"Well maybe the vocals were a little off that night. How about another beer?"

"Sure, what's your name yank?"

"Matthew, Mathew Baron. What's yours?"

"Kylie Cassidy."

I returned moments later with two icy cold Singha.

"So tell me Kylie, who was this guy on Bali with the Grateful Dead tapes?"

"About six or seven weeks ago I had arranged to meet some friends from back home at a small town on the southeast coast of Bali called Candidiasa. Within minutes of arriving there I find myself inside a reggae bar called The Legend Rock Cafe. At the bar I meet this guy named George, big as a mountain, with a long ponytail, sweet eyes and a sad smile. Since my friends weren't due to meet me for another few hours, I took him up on the opportunity to join him snorkeling. He said he was from California, and that he was 'on tour', because the guitarist from his favorite band had just died, and that he was having a tough time dealing with it. When I suggested to him that this seemed a little extreme, he told me that even though he had met him just once, he felt closer to... what was his name again?"

"Jerry, Jerry Garcia."

"George said that although he had met him just once, he felt closer to Jerry than to people that he had known his entire life. He said that through his music Jerry reached countless people in ways that just couldn't be explained. Personally I much prefer The Violent Femmes and Nick Cave."

I felt somewhat relieved to discover I wasn't the only person on the planet upset enough to uproot over Jerry's death. However, I was completely baffled and curious about this George, particularly of his use of the phrase 'shit sure and ready to tour'. My best friend Rich and I started saying this back in the seventies, whenever we were planning our numerous road trips to here, there and everywhere. One of us would say, "Blow out our speakers just one more time." To which the other would reply, "Shit sure and ready to tour." A small flame ignited in my belly. How could some total stranger be aware of our exclusive lingo?

"So George said to you, shit sure and ready to tour?"

"Yeah, that's what he said. He said he was off to an island in the south of Thailand called Kho Phangan to celebrate the full moon. Shit sure and ready to tour."

I spent the next few hours with Kylie drinking beers and eating chicken in green curry sauce. She was from a city in Australia called Woggawogga. She had been around the world almost twice, and wasn't in any rush to be home. She was taking pictures with disposable cameras and mailing them to her sister. She took my picture and told me I was on camera 211. We chatted through most of Conan, but watched the next film called *The Professional*. I had never seen it before and found it to be quite entertaining. Gary Oldman is in it, and he is riveting. I thought to myself, what a great actor Oldman was before he started making crap like Lost in Space. Anyway, in The Professional he plays a psycho, classical music loving cop gone bad to the max. At one point, when he tells another cop to bring him everyone, he screams to the questioning officer, EV REE ONE! When this happened, most of the people in the bar yelled in unison, EV REE ONE! It was very cool.

When The Professional ended, Kylie told me where I could get a room for the night. I exited the bar to find several Tuk-tuk drivers trying to talk me into taking a ride to Patpong, where all the prostitutes were putting on their shows. A vision popped into my head of myself explaining to the Scoopnecks how I had accidentally shared a case of Thai genital warts with their precious daughter Alexandra. I tugged at my collar and headed down the road to get a room.

As instructed by Kylie, I turned into the same alley that the two laughing youngsters had disappeared, and then veered left toward a small hole in the wall hotel. I registered and paid for two nights. I was in room 11 at the top of a narrow flight of stairs. I entered the four feet by eight feet room and turned on the fan that was screwed into the wall next to the three feet by seven feet bed. Down the hall I grabbed a cool shower, finishing with the full cold running on my somnolent head. I toweled off, hopped into bed, turned the fan toward my face and shut the light.

Half of my life
I spent doing time,
for some other fucker's crime
The other half found me
stumblin' around
drunk on burgundy wine

Tomorrow I would make some calls. After all there would be some explaining to do. I drew in a deep breath. The air smelled like cinnamon and bong water. Outside in the night I heard a group of people yell,

"EV REE ONE."

But I'll get back
on my feet some day
The good lord willing,
If he says I may

And who the hell is this George guy, and why is he saying 'shit sure and ready to tour', a phrase used by Rich, me, and nobody else. Weird stuff......

I know that the life,
I'm livin's no good
I'll get a new start,
Live the life I should

"Zzzzzz, zzzzzz..."

Boom, Boom,
Boom Boom Boom
Boom Boom Boom Boom

What the hell is that? Am I dreaming or what?

Boom Boom Boom
Bboom Bboom Boom

Either someone in the next room is pounding a bass or I'm caught in the Phil Zone. I banged on the wall a few times.

A voice from the other side called out, "Relax mate, we're almost done."

I'll get up and fly away
I'll get up and fly away,
fly away
Boom

4 <u>italian ice</u>

I awoke to the familiar sounds of city clatter. Although it occurred rarely, I always enjoyed waking up before my alarm would sound. I struggled to think of what appointments I had that day, but my mind drew a blank. I rolled over to check the time. Seeing no clock I realized that I wasn't home in bed, but in a closet converted into a guestroom in Bangkok.

> **Look out of any window**
> **any morning, any evening,**
> **any day**
> **Maybe the sun is shining**
> **birds are winging**
> **or rain is falling**
> **from a heavy sky -**
> **What do you want me to do?**
> **To do for you**
> **to see you through?**
> **This is all a dream we dreamed**
> **one afternoon long ago**

I reached for my Case Logic CD case and popped *Eat A Peach* into my Sony Walkman. I pressed play and advanced to track four, "Mountain Jam". I pulled on my headphones and lay back. On the ceiling above me someone had written, 'I fucked your Mama.' And below that someone had countered, 'Go home Dad, you're drunk.' I closed my eyes.

As the music started, I drifted off into a light sleep. I dreamed that I was at the Fillmore East in 1970 watching the original Allman Brothers Band. In reality, I was only 10 years old when these historic shows occurred, but here I was fully grown, watching the long dead Duane Allman and Berry Oakley reach unparalleled musical highs accompanied by the four surviving originals. A hand entered my field of vision, passing me a lit joint which I happily accepted. As the hand drew away I noticed that the middle finger was missing the top two digits. I drew deeply on the joint and watched myself turn my head to gaze upon none other than Captain Trips himself, Jerry Garcia. I exhaled a cloud of smoke and passed back the joint. I said, "Jerry, what are you doing here? You should be up in heaven."

Jerry accepted the joint and took a hit. He said, "Nowhere you can be that isn't where you're meant to be. It's easy."

He handed me back the joint, which I passed on to the next person. He was huge. It was Conan the Barbarian. He growled at the smoke and shook his head in disapproval. He rumbled, "I'll be back." Then he left.

I looked back at Jerry who shrugged and returned to enjoying the music. I took another hit off the joint and passed it to the next person. He too was huge. It was former NBA great and deadhead Bill Walton. Without taking a hit he passed the joint on. He bent way down and said, "No thanks. I would, but I'm training for the Olympic Snowboarding team." In his other arm he was holding a snowboard.

On stage, Duane, Berry, Dickey Betts and Greg Allman put down their instruments as Jaimoe and Butch Trucks settled into their drum duet. Bill tapped my shoulder and handed me the joint. I took another hit and passed it to Jerry. Jerry smiled at me, held up his hand as if to say I've had enough, and started up the aisle. It was probably the first time in his life; make that death, that he had ever turned down a high.

I called out, "Jerry, where you going?"

He replied, "I gotta take a leak, man."

And like that, he was gone.

The sound of a thumping bass grooved into alignment with the already present rat-a-tat swish crash of the drums, but it was Allen Woody and not Berry Oakley on the stage. And then Greg and Dickey returned, not with Duane, but with Warren Haynes. The Jam forging ever onward; as it always will. The guitars reeled, emitting melodious red and orange particles of unsullied joy. I envisioned one of those pour the paint on the spinning square paper contraptions that you sometimes find at carnivals and state fairs. Paint flew everywhere until the entire auditorium was swallowed by a rainbow tsunami of mishmash Technicolor brilliance. The music swelled into a swirling wall of sheer power that corkscrewed me out of my seat, high into the air. I was flying! I circled the multicolor audience once, and zoomed out an exit door into the street. Strangely, I was no longer in New York City. I was on Khao San Road in Bangkok. I landed kerplop in a gigantic container of chicken in green curry sauce, nose to nose with Conan. Somewhere, someone burped, so I quickly placed my right thumb to my forehead. Then Kylie Cassidy appeared and smacked Conan on his head. He collapsed into the slop and disappeared. Kylie helped me from the container and said, "Once in a while you can get shown the light in the strangest of places if you look at it right."

Mountain Jam culminated with a thunderous finale. I reached over and shut my Walkman. Sitting up in my miniature bed I scratched my sweaty balls and pondered where I might find myself a cup of coffee.

> **Walk out of any doorway**
> **feel your way, feel your way**
> **like the day before**
> **Maybe you'll find direction**
> **around some corner**
> **where it's been waiting**
> **to meet you -**
> **What do you want me to do?**
> **to watch for you**
> **while you're sleeping?**
> **Well please don't be surprised**
> **when you find me dreaming too**

Downstairs someone was shouting. I pulled on my clammy clothes and set off to see who was causing such a racket. At the tiny front desk, wearing red briefs and a pair of leather Italian loafers stood a short hairy man with Brylcream greasy hair pulled tightly back into a short eurotrash ponytail. He was berating an even shorter Thai man repeatedly shouting, "Stronso, stronso, stronso."

The Thai man stood quietly listening, seemingly unbothered by the high-strung angry hotel patron. I approached the two men and asked, "What's the problem?"

In broken English the hairy man replied, "Thisa stronso, he takesa my clothesa to the washa, anda nowa he saysa he forgetsa wherea he takesa them."

I looked over at the Thai man who nonchalantly shrugged and calmly answered, "No pay po washy, no hap clothes."

The hairy man again started to yell, "Stronso, stronso, stronso."

Later on I found out that stronso is an Italian word that translates loosely into English meaning turd.

I interrupted, "Whoa pisano, why don't you just pay him what you owe him?"

He replied, "My dinera, she isa ina the banca. Howa can I geta the dinera whena hea hasa my clothesa?"

"Well how about if I pay him what you owe him, then together we can go to the bank and you can repay me?"

"Grazie, grazie signore."

I paid the Thai man with a twenty. His eyes lit up when he saw the American currency.

He handed the hairy Italian his clothes, which had been stashed beneath the front desk all along. He said to me, "Tenk you, no chench po dollah." He disappeared through a curtain into the back room behind the front desk.

While the Italian went upstairs to get dressed, I passed the time by checking out some brochures that described available activities during a visit to Thailand. There were trekking tours to the north, featuring elephant rides through the jungle and bamboo rafting down obscure rivers. To the south were inexpensive excursions to exotic islands, with beachfront huts as accommodations. In Bangkok there were day tours to holy temples, and night tours to Patpong One and Patpong Two, where the most unholy of sex shows and debauchery were available. One brochure actually showed a succession of pictures of a young Thai woman with a Louisville Slugger being worked up into her deep as a well twat. The final photo, a close up, revealed that the bat was an authorized signature George Brett model. I chuckled softly to myself and couldn't help but look more closely at the bat to check it for pine tar. With the exception of some Asiatic poon juice, it was clean. This time the home run will count.

The short hairy Italian finally appeared.

He was wearing a matching shirt and shorts combo with a repeating print of giraffes wearing sunglasses on roller skates against a neon yellow backing, and a different pair of leather Italian loafers. He held up his wallet and said, "Okay, nowa we go toa the banco. Whatsa you namea?"

"Matthew, Matthew Baron, and what's your name?"

"I'ma Luigi Giancarlo Antonio de la Parma. Buta pleasea my frienda, calla me Ghiaccio." He stretched up his diminutive frame, held his head high and continued, "One daya I willa be asa famoosa asa the greata Pavarotti. Buta I noa singa the opera. I singa the hipa hopa anda the rapa musica. I willa be famoosa arounda the worlda as 'Ghiaccio, The Greata Italian Ice'. Whatsa you namea againa?"

"Matthew, you can call me Matt."

We stepped out into the narrow alley and after a few lefts and rights were on Khao San Road. Whereas last evening the sidewalks had been quiet, now they were jam packed with pedestrians, and merchants selling trinkets, clothes, jewelry and crap galore from around the world. Then I spotted a small cafe and suggested to Ghiaccio that we get some coffee before going to the bank. He replied that the coffee everywhere outside of Italy is shit. However, he knew of a special place, nearby, where the coffee god served the real thing. Although I was totally jonesing for a cup - RIGHT NOW - I agreed to wait. Moments later we entered the bank. While Ghiaccio withdrew some money, I exchanged my remaining U.S. currency into Thai baht. I would no longer pay twenty dollars in exchange for less costly items, as unscrupulous Thai merchants exclaimed, "No chench po dollah." With our banking finished we were off to visit the coffee god.

I followed Ghiaccio through a new maze of alleys, and was soon standing in front of a pushcart with an espresso machine sitting on top. A long electric cord ran from the machine up the side of a dilapidated building and into a window at the third floor. A line of people about forty deep waited patiently as, one by one, the coffee god filled orders. I guestimated that it would be about two hours before any caffeine would enter my body. This completely bummed me out. Then the voice of what must have been a coffee angel called out, "Matthew, over here, hurry up mate we're next."

It was Kylie from last night, and she was next on line. Ghiaccio and I stepped into the queue. Of course some of the international caffeine crazed people behind us started to grumble, but fortunately nobody cared all that much. Soon I was blessed with a long black, which in American coffee terminology translates into a quadruple espresso. Mmmmmm….. caffeine.

With coffee in hand the three of us headed back to Kao San Road to find food. Kylie recommended a cafe she knew called Thai One On. Before long we were eating large inexpensive plates of pad thai, and sharing stories about our lives.

> **Look into any eyes**
> **you find by you, you can see**
> **clear through to another day**
> **I know it's been seen before**
> **through other eyes**
> **on other days**
> **while going home**
> **What do you want me to do**
> **to do for you**
> **to see you through?**
> **It's all a dream we dreamed**
> **one afternoon long ago**

Kylie as I've already mentioned was from Woggawogga in Australia. She had finished high school and was working in a bakery when one rainy day a guy named Stefan from Sweden cruised into town in a beat up blue and white Volkswagen bus. He was spending the cold Swedish winter in the Southern hemisphere. Surfing and music were his passions. He had flown into Melbourne to see Pearl Jam, and had won the bus hustling pool. His plans were to drive up the East Coast and hit as many surf beaches along the way as he could. From there he was off to Bali and beyond. He had pierced nipples and a tattoo of Jimi Hendrix on the side of his shaven head. According to Kylie he was passing through Woggawogga because he had heard that they had the best cherry pie in the world. I suppose Kylie was his proof of that. Two days later when that beat up VW left town, so did Kylie. She hadn't been back since.

Ghiaccio was from the small coastal town of Fiumiccino, just outside of Rome. It was his dream to be a superstar rap singer. When MTV broke through onto European television, Vanilla Ice with his hit "Ice Ice Baby" was all the rage. That's when Luigi ceased to exist, and Ghiaccio, or Italian Ice was born. He had just spent the past summer touring Italy, France, and Spain, playing at clubs along the Riviera with his band, Ghiaccio e Gli Signore d'caldo. His rap went like this:

Ghiaccio, ghiaccio Bambina
ghiaccio, ghiaccio Bambina
I'ma Italian Ice
I'ma quite a guy
Don'ta aska why
Cause Im'a very shy
But when it comesa to romancin'
Anda Hipa Hopa dancin'
I'ma melt you freaky
Like a parmigiana cheesy
I ain'ta no Mussolini
Witha hair thatsa greasy
My raps a facil easy
So pretty pleasa please me
ghiaccio, ghiaccio Bambina
ghiaccio, ghiaccio Bambina

Fortunately for Ghiaccio his father owned a company that sold a lot of expensive leather shoes and accessories. And although I doubted that his music was going to take him very far, his readily apparent self-confidence and determination came shining through when he spoke. In essence, chasing his dream looked good on him.

My own story about working in New York City as an attorney was boring to me, but seemed interesting enough to Kylie and Ghiaccio. I was elaborating about my East 12th street apartment and Park Avenue office when

I experienced another reality check. Here I was sitting in a cafe in Bangkok, 2-3 days late for work, depending on what side of the planet you happen to be on, all because Jerry was dead. I signaled to the waiter to bring the check. I needed to touch base with the real world in New York, but first I needed to score some clothing more suited to the oppressive temperature outside.

Walk into splintered sunlight
Inch your way
through dead dreams
to another land
Maybe you're tired and broken
Your tongue is twisted
with words half spoken
and thoughts unclear
What do you want me to do
to do for you
to see you through
A box of rain will ease the pain
and love will see you through

Kylie and Ghiaccio joined me as I entered one of the seemingly endless clothing bazaars that inhabit Kao San Road. Whereas each bazaar sold its own flavor of sarongs, shorts and shirt combos, inexpensive leather items and shoes, the one item they all had in common was a vast selection of Bob Marley memorabilia. As I later discovered in my travels, the great Ganja Bob and his music and message are an ever growing worldwide phenomenon. His t-shirts, cassettes, CDs, books, and posters are sold virtually everywhere. I selected a Rasta man Vibration t-shirt and a pair of lightweight cotton drawstring shorts. I also purchased a daypack that I stuffed with my saturated skunky clothes.

"How can I telephone the United States," I asked my two new friends?

"There's an international calling center just down the road," answered Kylie. "All you do is give them the number you want to call and then pay them at the finish."

Kylie and Ghiaccio walked me to the telephone center. Kylie then excused herself as she had some packing to do. She had made plans to leave early the next morning on a trekking tour up north in the mountains of Chiang Mai. She said I could meet her later that evening at Hello Bar. Ghiaccio then excused himself to go take a nap at the hotel. He said that he wanted to "catcha siesta" so that he would be rested for later when he would venture into the sweaty seediness that is Patpong 2.

Once inside the telephone center I found a booth and phoned my apartment to retrieve my messages. There were six. Two from my boss, 'The Rajah', inquiring about my whereabouts. One from Lisa informing me that one of the partners, Mr. Spilatti, was asking for me. Two from my mother, one telling me to call her right away as she was concerned about my behavior the other night, and the other sounding even more distraught because neither Alexandra, nor Lisa, nor Rich knew of my whereabouts. The final call was from Rich saying, "Your mom douches with Drano, your pop looks like Lou Costello. Tell me buddy, how's the ole' tomato. Scratch the middle for me. Are you on tour?"

Alexandra hadn't left a message. I questioned if she knew I was away. I questioned if she cared. I questioned whether I cared if she cared.

> **Just a box of rain -**
> **wind and water -**
> **Believe it if you need it,**
> **if you don't just pass it on**
> **Sun and shower -**
> **Wind and rain -**
> **in and out the window**
> **like a moth before a flame**

"Hello mom."

"Matthew, where are you, I've been so worried."

"Mom, don't worry. I'm fine. I'm in Bangkok."

"Bangkok? What in god's name are you doing in China?"

"Actually mom, Bangkok is in Thailand. I need a break from things at home. I need some time to do a little soul searching."

"Soul searching? What about your job? What about your apartment? What about your future with Alexandra? What am I going to tell your father?" Mom was beginning to unravel. "When are you coming home?"

"Calm down mom, everything is fine, really." Of course I had no idea what I was going to do. "As soon as I'm off the phone with you I'll call Lisa. She can handle all the details concerning my job, my apartment, and anything else that needs to be handled. As for now, I'm going to take a little time to reflect upon my life. As for dad, tell him to bet on the Yankees, I've got a feeling they're going to get hot. I love you. Bye" Click.

I dialed the office.

"You have reached the office of Matthew Baron at the law firm of Goldberg, Greenberg, Trachtenberg, Ditkoff, Kowalicek, Brannigan, Spilatti, and De Nunzio." It was Lisa's voice on the answering machine. "Our office is presently closed. Please leave a message at the tone and we will return your call during regular office hours. Thank you." I later found out that I was calling New York at 3:00 in the morning the previous day. My mother in all her upset had neglected to mention the time.

"Hello Lisa, its Matthew. I'm in Bangkok...Thailand. I'll call back to explain. Tell Roger and anyone else who asks that I had an emergency, the death of a close friend. Tell them I'll be out of town for a few days. Thanks." Click.

"Hello," a sleepy female voice answered Rich's telephone.

"Let me speak with Rich please. It's urgent. Tell him it's Mr. Hunt from the census bureau. Ask him if he's seen my son Mike."

"Rich, wake up, it's urgent. There's a guy on the phone from the census bureau. He needs to know if you've seen Mike Hunt."

Rich had already taken the phone. Over

my laughter he grumbled, "Evening Mr. Hunt. You're a class act. What's the big idea interrupting my post fornication beauty rest? And you better call your momma, cause she called here last night and she's about to shit a mandel loaf. Where you at, Cletus?"

"I'm in Bangkok."

"Bangkok! Amazing!! What the hell are you doing in Bangkok?"

"I started thinking about Jerry's death the other night and I just had to do something..., anything. You know, like when those dragon blotters we ate at Englishtown kicked in and you had to keep on jumping until the grass cooled down. And by the way, who's the debutante?"

"What an unusual time to be inquiring about my cousin Deb. She's been spending a lot of time down south, trawling for olives in the brush. But enough of her, what did you tell the brass down at the firm?"

"I left a message saying that a friend had died. That should cover me for a few days. After that, well, I haven't gotten that far yet."

"And what about Alexandra?"

"I haven't spoken with her since I left. She hasn't even left a message for me on my machine. Well, fuck it all. I'm in Bangkok. I might as well enjoy myself. Even if my entire life back at home turns to shit in a matter of days."

"That's the spirit. Sounds like you're on tour."

"I'm glad you brought that up. The first night I'm here, I start talking to this Australian chick. She tells me that about a month ago she was talking to this large pony tailed guy named George from California who said to her, shit sure and ready to tour. Do you know this guy?"

"Beats me, what else do you know about him?"

"Only that like me, Jerry's death made such a strong impression on him that he also picked up and hit the road."

"The whole thing sounds kind of cosmic. How would some stranger be onto our lingo? Where's this George now?"

"I don't know. According to Kylie he was heading to some island called Kho Phangan for a full moon party. But that was about a month ago."

"So what now?"

"Well my gut is telling me that maybe I should do a little island hopping and see if I can locate this joker. I mean what the hell, I might as well, I am in Thailand."

"Eeyup, might as well, might as well. Good luck and remember to call your mom. And when you do, be sure to remind her that I need back the loafers I left under her bed the other night."

"Get a new line already, that one's as old as your father's subscription to Boy's Life."

"Later."

"Later." Click

It's just a box of rain
I don't know who put it there
Believe it if you need it
or leave it if you dare
But it's just a box of rain
or a ribbon for your hair
Such a long long time
to be gone
and a short time
to be there

5 shit sure and ready to tour

I entered Hello Bar just as the movie *The Lion King* was finishing. After disposing of his evil Uncle Scar, the newly empowered King Simba strides to the top of Pride Rock to roar with satisfaction as he fulfills his destiny in the great circle of life. Then Elton John began to sing. I ordered a double scotch. As I sipped, I contemplated my own place in the great circle of life; my existence in New York City, my job, my friends, my family, my engagement to a woman that I was unsure of my love, and what I was now doing in Bangkok. No answers came, but I decided that maybe I should search for some.

> **Inspiration, move me brightly,**
> **light the song**
> **with sense and color,**
> **hold away despair**
> **More than this I will not ask**
> **faced with mysteries**
> **dark and vast**
> **statements just seem**
> **vain at last**
> **some rise, some fall,**
> **some climb**
> **to get to Terrapin**

"Matta, howsa ita goinga?"

"Hey Ghiaccio."

"I'ma goingta watcha the nexta filma, you eva seea the una flewova the acuckoosa nest?"

"Sure, I've seen it lots of times."

Actually, in a roundabout way, *One Flew Over the Cuckoo's Nest* is what introduced me to attending Grateful Dead concerts. Back in high school English class, Rich and I had to do a book report on a novel written by a contemporary American author. A few years earlier the movie version of cuckoo's nest had swept the Academy awards. Since Rich and I thought the movie was such a blast, we chose to read the novel for our book report. However, when Rich's dad caught wind of this he inquired if we knew anything about the book's author, Ken Kesey? When we told him that we had never heard of Kesey, he recommended that we consider doing our report on a different book called *The Electric Kool Aid Acid Test*. Since Morton Reiner was very cool as dads go, after all he had introduced us to *The Allman Brothers Live at Fillmore East* and numerous Frank Zappa records, we decided to do our report on Tom Wolfe's acid test. Not only did the book open our minds to the possibility of 'getting on the bus', it also introduced us to The Merry Prankster's own house band, the Grateful

Dead. That summer at the Englishtown Raceway we saw our first Dead show; a full day experience of better living through chemistry and music, featuring the New Riders of the Purple Sage, the Marshall Tucker Band and of course, the Grateful Dead.

"Gidevenin Matt" said Kylie.

"Good evening Kylie." I didn't try to copy her Aussie accent.

"I'm all packed and ready for four days of trekking in the mountains of Chiang Mai. Tomorrow at this time, after a day of riding elephants through the jungle, I'll be drinking Mekong whiskey and smoking opium under the stars with the locals. And how about you, have you made any plans?"

"Well, I called back to New York and spoke to some people. And since I'm pretty much an open book right now, I figured I'd see if I could locate this George that you had mentioned. What do you think the chances are that he's still on Kho Phangan?"

"I really couldn't say. But the full moon is in another two nights. Maybe he enjoyed himself enough at the last party to return again for this month's blowout."

**Counting stars by candlelight
all are dim but one is bright:
the spiral light of Venus
rising first and shining best,
From the northwest corner
of a brand new crescent moon
crickets and cicadas sing
a rare and different tune
Terrapin Station**

"So how can I get to Kho Phangan," I asked? "How long will it take?"

Kylie answered, "Go to any of the local travel agencies. They can book it for you. It takes about half a day by train and ferry."

**in the shadow of the moon
Terrapin Station
and I know we'll be there soon**

"Once I'm there, how would I go about finding George?"

"I'm not sure, but if I were you I'd go to a beach called Haadrin. That's where the major partying takes place. There will be all night raves with plenty of good medicine. You'll probably arrive too late to get a hut or a room, but there's sure to be lots of people crashing on the beach."

Terrapin-I can't figure out
Terrapin-if it's an end
or the beginning
Terrapin-but the train's
got its brakes on
and the whistle is screaming:
Terrapin

Shit sure and ready to tour. I was on my way to Kho Phangan to search out the mysterious George.

6 <u>sway</u>

The next morning I booked passage to Kho Phangan. That evening I would catch an overnight train to Surat Thani in the south, and then an early morning bus would connect me with a ferry which would drop me off around noon on the island. With nothing to pack I found myself lounging at Hello bar with the rest of the world travelers. I ordered some pad thai and a beer. Someone belched. I raised my right thumb to my forehead. I chuckled along with the crowd as some muscular German guy with a Billy Idol bleached look got smacked on the head. At first he was a little angry, but he quickly calmed down once the game was explained to him.

My food arrived just as the first film of the day began. Titled, *My Life As A Dog*, this film made in Sweden is quite funny even if you don't understand Swedish. Of course the four beers I consumed didn't hurt any.

The next film was *Legends of the Fall*. I had already slept through this film on my flight over to Bangkok. On screen a bear growls. I yawn. I'm not even past the opening credits and I'm fading fast.
Growl...yawn...zzzzzzzzzzzzzz

In the attics of my life
Full of cloudy dreams unreal
Full of tastes no one can know
And lights no eye can see
When there was no ear to hear
You sang to me

Zzzzzzsssssssstanley, The Stanley Theatre in Pittsburgh. I'm dreaming that I'm standing front row center, March 6, 1981 watching Phil Lesh adjust his synchrotron. I bellow, "PHILLLLL," but he is too absorbed to notice. Standing next to me is my lifelong friend Teddy Fitz, or as he was known in high school Teddy Quah, because of his love of Hot Tuna. This is Teddy's first Dead show and my first time in the front row. We snort a few spoons of blow and pound the stage in anticipation. One by one the band saunters on stage. Bobby counts one, two, three, and in unpretentious, unfettered unison the Dead serenely accelerate into Jack Straw. Dressed in black t-shirt and brown corduroy pants just a few feet away stands Jerry, stoically milking sweet notes from his guitar. He peers out over the top of his glasses at the already ecstatic electric throng of dancing enchanted crazies, void of emotion, gently rocking to and fro, doing his job, pleasing the masses. Song after song I watch in amazement as he effortlessly fingers note after glorious note, never pushing the issue, never overplaying. The rest of the band complementing him, at the expense of sounding cliché, perfectly. While the music plays the band. Toward the finish of the first set "Let It Grow" flows into "Deal". And as Deal builds up into a feverish repetition of the catchphrase 'Don't you let that deal go down,' I make eye contact with Jerry. He gazes into my eyes for a second or two, his expression never changing, only to refocus out into the crowd. 'Don't you let that deal go down, Don't you let that deal go down, oh no.' And then the unimaginable happens. Jerry pushes off and actually leaves the stage, airborne by all of maybe1/2 inch...

"EV REE ONE." I awake with a startle. For the second time in a week I had slept through *Legends of the Fall*. *The Professional* was in progress with the crowd complementing Gary Oldman, dare I say, perfectly.

My train would leave in about three hours. I decided to buy another change of clothes, this time settling for a stylin' blue batik shirt, and another pair of cotton shorts. I also bought a swimsuit, some sun protection, and a pair of Revo knockoffs. I gathered my few possessions at the hotel and made it back to Hello Bar for dinner. I washed down another plate of pad thai with a few beers, anxious about my imminent journey, pleased with myself for making the foolhardy effort to find the mysterious George. *The Incredible Lightness of Being* was now playing on the TV, and although the plot didn't hold my attention, anytime Juliette Binoche came on screen I couldn't help but get a boner.

> **I have spent my life**
> **Seeking all that's still unsung**
> **Bent my ear to hear the tune**
> **And closed my eyes to see**
> **When there were**
> **no strings to play**
> **You played to me**

I boarded the train and found my accommodations. Along the walls of the train, above the level of the seats, were narrow Murphy type bunks with thin mattresses that the train attendants had folded down. Anyone with a little extra money could travel reclining, while the rest of the passengers passed the evening sleeping erect in the seats below. I climbed onto my sleeper and stretched out. I pulled out my Walkman and popped in *Sticky Fingers*. I skipped past "Brown Sugar", as I nearly always do, to the second song on the album, "Sway". As I listened my thoughts turned to that magical day a few years back on Maui, when I finally discovered the lyrics to this underrated, mostly missed, amazing Jagger/Richards composition.

For years, even decades, I had listened to Sway without the faintest idea of what Mick was singing. And even with only a vague understanding of the lyrics, the tune itself is so captivating, so mesmerizing, that it has forever held me clenched in the palm of its sweaty fist. Then one day while on vacation on Maui the solution to this long unsolved riddle settled serendipitously into my life. I was driving along the Hana Highway with a hitchhiker that I had picked up in Hookipa, where the windsurfing gods perform their special brand of wind and wave insanity. The hitchhiker's name was Gil. He was an aspiring musician who had traveled to Maui to explore the tropical weather and sweet, sweet sticky buds. We were cruising along enjoying 'the kine' when the song "Gimme Shelter" started playing on the radio of my metallic blue Mustang convertible rent-a-car. Gil began to sing along, and although he could carry a tune pretty well, I was more impressed that he actually knew all the words. I pulled the car over and half-hoping asked, "Do you know the Rolling Stones song, Sway?"

Gil replied, "Sure do."

My voice cracked as I asked, "Do you

know the lyrics?"

Gil repeated, "Sure do."

I couldn't believe it. "Tell them to me, please." And he did. "Write them down for me, please." And he did.

I had looked in music stores, asked countless Stones fans, even researched the Carnegie Hall Library of Music with no success. How satisfying, my quest to find the words to Sway was finally over. Thanks again, Gil. And as amazing as Sway is without a clue as to what Mick is singing, it becomes infinitely more powerful once the lyrics can be understood.

Sway(M. Jagger/K. Richards)
Did you ever wake up to find

There must be ways to find out

It's just that demon life
has got me in its sway

I hit the repeat button over and over,
listening to Sway countless times before
nodding off into a deep morpheun sleep.

In the book
of love's own dream
Where all the print is blood
Where all the pages
are my days
And all my lights grow old
When I had no wings to fly
You flew to me

I dreamed I was trekking along a winding
trail through a lush jungle. It was raining so
hard that all I could see was rain, green, and
my waterlogged, red canvas, high top Chuck
Taylor All-stars. Off in the distance I heard
people laughing. I forged on, slogging through
the mud, until the trail opened up into a small
clearing. Under a parachute used as a tarp,

surrounding a circular wooden table, illuminated by an enormous lava lamp in its center, sat five people: Bob Marley, Graham Chapman of Monty Python, two girls that I attended summer camp with in the seventies named Hazel 'Iron hands' Mapleton and Betty Ann 'Bigtits' Felgus, and a large pony tailed man that I intuitively recognized as the mysterious George. I sat down in the one available seat. Bob handed me a dry towel to wipe the water from my face. He said, "Open your eyes and look within. Are you satisfied with the life your living?"

I looked into his eyes and felt his power, and his warmth. I was too awestruck to answer.

The rain spontaneously stopped. George said to me, "Good to see you after all these years."

I replied, "Have we met before?"

George answered, "Before what?" When I hesitated to answer, George chuckled, "Don't think so hard. Let's have a smoke."

He produced three large spliffs from his shirt pocket and lit them. He passed one left to Hazel, one right to Graham and kept the third for himself. I asked, "George, have you seen

Jerry?"

He sadly shook his head and replied, "Nope, but he lives in here." He patted his hand over his heart. "And in here." He patted his boom box.

Hazel asked Betty Ann, "Who was the guy that sang that apple pie song where the guy drives his truck to somewhere, but then this other guy dies?"

I instantly downshifted into Jeopardy mode, buzzed in and stated, "What is "American Pie" by Don McLean?"

Whereupon Graham took a swig from a bottle of Captain Morgan's spiced rum and belligerently added, "Donovan would never sing that shite."

By now the two spliffs had made their way around the circle back to George. He added the two burning fattys to the one already in his mouth and inhaled deeply, drawing in a gargantuan hit from all three at once. He followed this feat with a double chug-a-lug from the rum. His eyes shot open wide and he exhaled a monstrous smoke cloud that impressed even Bob. He broke into a grin of satisfaction, then turning to Graham said, "That may be true, but he did sing "Hurdy Gurdy"."

Everyone broke out laughing.

"C'mon kids," said George, rising from his chair, "let's go dance and shake our bones."

Everyone single filed out the back trail from the site. We came to a road where a blue and white VW bus sat. Behind the wheel was Stefan from Norway. I could tell by his Hendrix tattoo. Next to him sitting shot-gun was Kylie from Woggawogga. We all piled in and took off. Within seconds the bus began climbing these incredibly steep switchbacks. Outside the window of the bus we were engulfed by a bazillion stars. Kylie fiddled with the radio dial, passing the songs Jack Straw, Sway, American Pie and Hurdy Gurdy before settling on of all things Whitney Houston singing "I Will Always Love You". The two girls in back starting singing, or more like howling along. George lit another spliff. Bob sat peacefully, and Graham grumbled to himself about what a wanker Don McLean was. Before long the bus stopped in front of Winterland in San Francisco. George looked my way. There was lightning in his eyes. He said, "Surat Thani."

I awoke to the rumbling and scuffling of passengers leaving the train. I grabbed my things and made way for the bus that would take me to the ferry. Since the inside of the bus was packed full, I was obliged to ride on the outside with several Thai locals, latching on to an open window while balancing precariously on the bumper. Hanging on like a Fall leaf. Fortunately, it was a short trip and the road wasn't rough. Upon arrival, brown water resembling coffee was available at the dock, and I was soon seaward on my way to Kho Phangan.

You flew to me

As the ferry cruised along, my thoughts were of my dream meeting with George. I sure hoped he would be on Kho Phangan so that I could speak with him about Jerry's death, and find out why he was saying 'shit sure and ready to tour'. I gazed out over the blue expanse of the Gulf of Thailand. Transposed against a few wispy clouds, far off in the sky appeared an image of myself standing at the altar, waiting for Alexandra. All my friends and relatives were present. All eyes were upon me. Alexandra started down the aisle. Over her shoulder in the distance were the two blonde dancers from the Red Rocks concert, spinning round and round and round. I wanted to join the dancing lovelies, but my feet wouldn't move. I was wearing concrete shoes. Alexandra reached out to take my hand. Her hand was a vice clamp.

In the secret space of dreams
Where I dreaming lay amazed
When the secrets all are told
And the petals all unfold
When there was
no dream of mine
You dreamed of me

It's just that demon life has got me in its sway.

*Lyrics to Sway, by Mick Jagger and Keith Richards, not used in this chapter in their entirety, as ABKCO would not give permission without hefty compensation. Hey ABKCO, "You suck!"

7 scrape scrape scrape

I arrived on Kho Phangan where the ferry was met by an open bed shuttle truck that drove me and about fifteen other assorted travel types to Haadrin Beach. A very tan German fellow working with the Shuttle Company answered questions as the truck pitched and rolled over the uneven dirt road. His advice on finding accommodations was to avoid the beach, and grab anything that might be available in the small town just beyond the palm trees. When the truck stopped, I ignored his advice and started straight for the beach. My life experiences had taught me that when everyone heads in one direction, that it is in my best interests to go the complete opposite way. Sure enough, just as I approached Haadrin Beach I spotted two travelers helping a third very ill traveler toward the soon to be departing shuttle truck.

I asked, "What happened to him?"

The sick fellow squinted at me through glassy eyes and moaned.

"Dengue fever, real bad," answered one of the healthy fellows.

"Where was he staying?" I inquired, hoping to get lucky.

The other healthy fellow answered, "Over that way, in cabin number nine, but you don't want to stay there, it's cursed. He's the second person in a row to stay there that has caught the fever."

Haadrin Beach was a tranquil quarter mile cove of beautiful white sand, sparsely sprinkled by small clusters of topless sunbathers. The blue water lapped gently at the shore while swimmers frolicked in the scorching afternoon sun. I approached the nearby group of cabins, and was soon speaking with the manager who said that he knew nothing of a curse, and would be happy to rent me the newly vacant number nine on the beach.

The wheel is turning
and you can't slow down
You can't let go
and you can't hold on
You can't go back
and you can't stand still
If the thunder don't get you
then the lightning will

I unlocked the door to my cursed cabin and hesitantly peered inside. Seeing no friends of the devil, I walked lightly across the creaking wooden floor, and cautiously sat down on the mosquito net covered bed. As an extra precaution I recited the only spell I knew, from an old *Munster's* episode, in order to exorcise any invisible dengue demons that might exist.

"Alacazam and acey dosey
Abracadabra and Bela Lugosi"

I chuckled to myself at my juvenile behavior, but somehow found comfort in my ridiculous attempt to rid my cabin of its curse. I took an ice cold shower, pulled on my new swim trunks, and headed out for some lunch, high with anticipation, optimistic that I might locate George.

A short distance from my cabin was an empty volleyball court. Next to the court was a small bar where several people sat enjoying cold drinks. Just behind the bar was a restaurant of sorts called Cafe A. Playing on a TV next to the register was the movie *Steel Magnolias*. I sat down at a small table facing out toward the beach and waited. Within a few minutes a young Thai girl brought a menu. I ordered a ham and cheese jaffle, which is basically a grilled sandwich, and a large iced tea. I glanced at the TV and was aghast to see Daryl Hannah looking so bad that they must have been filming on the day that JFK Jr. told her that her chances of becoming a Kennedy were about as promising as the Red Sox chances of winning the World Series.

"Excuse me," inquired a longhaired guy in boxers who was in the company of two attractive young women in bikinis. "Would it be all right if we joined you?"

I answered, "Sure. Be my guest."

"My name is Antony," said the longhaired guy, "and these lovelies are my friends, Sue and Jill." Both girls said hello. "I was wondering if you needed anything special for tomorrow night?"

I looked over at the two girls. "What exactly are you offering?"

Antony and the girls laughed, and then he responded, "Oh no, nothing like that. I mean for your head, For the full moon. I've got X, shrooms, grass, speed, you name it."

The waitress brought my lunch.

"Well actually, I haven't made up my mind yet. Maybe I can let you know later. However, by any chance do you know a friend of mine, a big, longhaired guy, American, who goes by the name George? He was here for the last full moon."

Jill responded, "You must be talking about mushroom George, with the big sad eyes. Is that the George you mean?"

Optimistically I continued, "Well that sounds like it could be him. He was probably traveling with music by a band called the Grateful Dead. They're his favorite."

"That's him," said Sue.

"Well all right!" My pleasure at locating George was quite evident. "Do you know where I can find him?"

My glee was short-lived.

"Didn't he say he was off to Bali," Antony inquired of the girls? They both nodded in agreement. "Must have been about a week ago or so. I think he said he was going to hook up with some friends back in Bangkok, and then he was off to check out the full moon in some small town on Bali. I can't remember the name."

"Candidiasa," I questioned?

"I think that was it," said Sue. "He mentioned something about spending the next full moon in a much more laid back fashion. You know, as opposed to drinking mushroom tea and dancing until the sun comes up."

As I ate my lunch, my companions who were from Cape Town, South Africa shared their own travel story, and how they came to know George. Antony and Sue were an item, and Jill was Sue's younger sister. They had left Cape Town just after Antony had completed his degree in Architectural Design. Sue and Jill were from a wealthy family who were footing the bill for all their travels. Sue was a free spirit and completely unconcerned about her future. Jill was an aspiring photographer who dreamed of one day finding her Paul McCartney. They had been back and forth between Kho Phangan, Phuket, and several other Thai islands, scuba diving, partying, basically living a hedonistic lifestyle. At the last full moon they came across George. He had a huge bag of mushrooms that he was sharing with anyone that wanted to partake. Every time someone would chomp some down, so would he. He had told them that if he ate enough mushrooms, then he might meet up with a faraway friend he was hoping to find. However, when they saw him a few days later and asked him if he ever saw his friend, he had sadly replied, no. For the next two or three weeks he just hung around getting high, listening to his music, and teaching people to play Ultimate Frisbee.

> **Won't you try**
> **just a little bit harder?**
> **Couldn't you try**
> **just a little bit more?**
> **Won't you try**
> **just a little bit harder?**
> **Couldn't you**
> **try just a little bit more?**

Although I was certainly intrigued at spending the coming full moon on this island paradise, my quest to locate George was my immediate priority. I caught the next shuttle back to the ferry, and was happily surprised to find out that Surat Thani had its own puny little airstrip with connecting flights to Denpassar, a city on Bali. I bought a ticket for the next departing flight. The plane resembled a school bus with wings. By sunset I was riding a rented Kawasaki 110 rice burner into the city of Sanur Beach on Bali. Tomorrow morning I would be on my way to Candidiasa.

Round round robin run around
Gotta get back
where you belong
Little bit harder,
just a little bit more
Little bit farther
than you've gone before

Sanur Beach was a mostly undeveloped beach town with several big hotel chains, all offering paradise waterfront accommodations at inflated rates. I cruised the streets for a short while before checking into the moderately priced, off the beaten path, Bali Senia Resort Guesthouse. The hotel manager, whose name was Ketut, led me up two flights of beautifully polished, white marble stairs, and into an amazing guest room filled with Balinese art and a hand carved teke bed. Through adjacent double doors was an open-air veranda with the same marble floors and exquisite red velvet couches covered with silk throw pillows. Across the way, on the roof at the other end of the hotel, standing about ten feet high was an impressive stone temple.

I walked into town and found a lone hole in the wall restaurant. I ordered some papaya juice, and some rice and vegetables. When my order was ready I heard someone in the kitchen call out, "Ketut." The waiter walked to the kitchen to pick up my order. I pondered the coincidence that the only two names that I had heard on all of Bali were identical. Perhaps Bali ran parallel with a dream I had years ago when everyone in the world looked like actor John Cazale, best known for playing Fredo in the Godfather movies. However, no such circumstance existed, as I later discovered that it is a Balinese tradition to name your first son Ketut. On Bali, there are Ketuts everywhere.

Ketut the waiter placed my food and drink in front of me. The papaya juice looked enticingly electric and tasted extremely sweet and creamy. It was like no other beverage I had ever tasted. I thoroughly enjoyed every mouthful and ordered a second glass.

As tomorrow evening would bring the full moon, and I was fatigued from all the traveling, I returned to the guesthouse immediately after finishing my meal. I began climbing the polished steps that led to my room when I decided to pause at the top of the first flight to look down the hall. What I discovered was a long hallway tiled about one-third the way in the same white marble. The remainder of the floor was dirt. And how strange that all the rooms along the hall were without doors. I wondered if I was the only guest. I climbed to the next level and found this corridor to be the same. Although this seemed unusual, I didn't give it much thought. After all, Sanur Beach is just a small city on Bali, and they hadn't yet finished constructing the facility. I returned to my room and lay down selecting Talking Heads-*Fear of Music* for my Walkman. I fell asleep just as David Byrne sang, "Everything seems to be up in the air at this point....."

Sometime later I awoke to an unusual scraping noise. Scrape, scrape, scrape. Scrape, scrape, scrape. Scrape, scrape, scrape. Then the scraping stopped, but seconds later began again. Scrape, scrape, scrape. Scrape, scrape, scrape. I rose from my bed and walked out to the veranda. Over by the temple was the silhouette of a man, but I could not tell what was causing the scraping. I slipped on my Tevas, and made my way down the marble tiled hall, which soon changed to dirt. As I neared the temple I could distinguish in the moonlight the exquisite detail that had gone into the carving of the stones. How totally mind-blowing that this prodigious structure was erected way up high on the roof. It must have weighed tons.

Squatting next to the temple was a small brown man. In his hands he held a white marble tile, whose edge he was scraping against one of the large stones at the temple's base. He paused for a second to inspect the edge of the tile, then returned to his scraping. When he was finally satisfied with the tile's appearance he gently leaned it against several other white tiles. He then picked up a fresh tile and began scraping it against the temple. After watching him for a full minute or so, he looked my way. He smiled at me pleasantly, never pausing from his scraping. The entire moment was supersaturated in absurdity. Here I was, in the middle of the night, on a rooftop on Bali, watching some lunatic scrape tiles at the base of a totally improbable, preposterous temple.

Up in the sky, a helicopter chopped its way toward the beach. The man stopped his scraping and gathered up his tiles. He walked past me down the corridor, and disappeared into the open doorway of one of the rooms along the hall. Feeling a bit uneasy I followed him into the dimly lit room with the dirt floor, and into a slightly smaller room. Inside that room, working by candlelight alone, the man laid the tiles, building what I guessed by a few exposed pipes was going to become a bathroom. Meticulously he applied the mortar, and using two strings as a plumb and level, laid tile after tile. Somewhat bewildered and completely astounded, I watched him for about ten minutes in silence until he finished. Then he walked right past me, returning to the temple to begin scraping more tiles. Feeling overwhelmed by the increasingly surreal quality of the moment, I decided to return to my room. However, when I entered the stairwell my curiosity compelled me to follow the stairs up and explore whatever might be at the next level.

At the top of the stairs I proceeded through an unlocked teke door. Directly in front of me, in the center of the roof, stood a four-post canopy. Beneath the canopy was a bridge table with four chairs. Again a helicopter passed overhead. I thought to myself, how unusual for helicopters to be flying around in the middle of the night, especially in a place as remote as Sanur Beach. I monitored the path of the copter, watching in fascination as it rendezvoused with a second helicopter. Then the two helicopters rose higher and higher, until they seemed to be level with the stars, only to head off in opposite directions. Whereas one of the helicopters quickly disappeared along the horizon, the other made its way closer and closer to what appeared to be a golden oval shaped star. Then just as the two converged, the helicopter vanished, seemingly absorbed by the star. I stared at the beautiful star, mesmerized by its brightness and unfamiliarity. Then it began to descend. I watched in amazement as the golden orb followed a steady, deliberate path toward the

Earth. Eventually, when it was hovering about a mile or two off the coast, and maybe a hundred yards above the water, it stopped. A few tense seconds passed and the star emitted a laser of green light straight down toward the water. The light touched down on the water's surface and immediately sent a second alternating green light back up to the star. I gasped and quietly murmured to myself, "What the fuck?"

The only answer that made any sense was that I was witnessing an honest to god UFO. My first thought was that I must shoot some pictures, but how? I didn't have a camera with me, and there was no way that I was going to find a place to purchase one. I ran down the steps to the guesthouse office. It was locked and unattended. I explored the entire first floor and then the second to confirm that I was the only guest. I was. I ran back to the roof to be certain that I wasn't just imagining the entire situation. Sure enough, there was the star, or to be more accurate, the UFO. It was still doing its laser beam dance against the water, seemingly sending energy down, or more likely, drawing some kind of energy up.

Scrape, scrape, scrape.

I ran to the lunatic Indonesian nocturnal mason. I feverishly motioned for him to come with me, to follow me, but he wasn't the least bit interested. I continued to implore him, begging, "Come on, come with me up to the roof you lunatic, I've got to share this with someone. Come on, come on!"

He nonchalantly collected his tiles, brushed past me, and made his way back to his bathroom project. I ran to the roof, my heart pounding like Bill and Mickey at the beginning of "The Other One", Fillmore East, 2-11-69. I stood at the roof's edge watching in amazement when I spontaneously clapped my hands three times. The laser light beams stopped. The orb, which had changed to a reddish orange began moving toward me. I stood frozen, excited, thinking well this is it, E.T. here I come. The mysterious vessel came within a few hundred yards and then stopped. I held my breath. After a few seconds it started moving away, returning to its original destination. The beam of light resumed its dance with the water down below.

I ran to the unfinished bathroom. The lunatic was carefully placing his last tile into place. "Please, please come with me," I begged, my arms and expression trying to draw him in my direction. To him, I must have appeared to be a lunatic.

Finally, yielding to my desperation, he came. Up to the roof we went, where with great satisfaction I pointed to this extraordinary event. He watched for a few seconds, looked blankly my way, and calmly returned to his work.

I felt like the man in the fabled story who finds Picasso drawing in the sand with the tide coming in, and no way to save the masterpiece, or prove the moment. I sat on the roof and watched. In the distance I heard more scraping. Time moved slowly as my eyes grew heavy and I fought my body's will to get some sleep.

The light beam ceased and once again the orb, now blue indigo, slowly approached. When it was directly overhead a solid white light beam touched down engulfing the canopy and the table and chairs. Under me the entire building rumbled, just like Phil's bass as he joined Bill and Mickey on that same 1969 Fillmore East Other One. Appearing in three of the four chairs were Buddy Holly, Ritchie Valens, and J.P. Richardson, A.K.A. The Big Bopper. Petrified, I stood like David, searching for the courage to more closely examine my long extinguished distinguished guests. I somehow managed to not shit my shorts as I incredulously persuaded my feet to approach these reanimated pioneers of rock n roll. I stopped next to the one available chair.

J.P. extended his arm inviting me to join them.

Buddy smiled.

Ritchie said, "Relax man. Que pasa amigo?"

"Uhhhhhhhh, I don't know. What's happening with you guys?"

All three stood up. Magically, Buddy and Ritchie were holding guitars. They began to strum, and J.P. clapped along. Buddy abruptly stopped, saying, "Hold on there just one second boys." He quickly tuned his strings. "Okay now, let's try that again."

It was the day the music was resurrected. Again the little jam session began, and with the voices of angels they sang:

The wheel is turning
and you can't slow down
You can't let go
and you can't hold on
You can't go back
and you can't stand still
If the thunder don't get you
then the lightning will

I awoke alone on the roof. The mystery light was gone, and so was the evening's entertainment. The evening sky was just changing to dawn. All was silent, no scraping, no Bill, Mickey or Phil. I returned to my room and lay down. "The Other One" had been but a tease.

Small wind turn
by the fire and rod
Big wheel turn
by the grace of God
Every time
that wheel turn round
bound to cover
just a little more ground

Zzzzzzzzzzzzzzzzzzzzzzzzzzzzzzzzzzzzzzzzzzzz

Bound to cover
just a little more ground

8 comin' around

The morning sun peeked through my curtains illuminating a beautiful framed print of nearby Mount Batur. I gathered my possessions and headed out to greet the day. Across the expanse I spied the stone temple which loomed splendiferous in the distance. The previous evening's events sprinted through my brain. I contemplated going back to the roof, but decided in favor of another helping of magic papaya juice, and hopefully a cup of decent coffee. I hopped on my bike and headed for the same restaurant. A different waiter named Ketut took my order and was soon bringing me another serving of heaven in a glass. Tonight would bring the full moon, and maybe with some luck a meeting with George. Off I headed for Candidiasa. Shit sure and ready to tour.

> **The other day they waited,**
> **the sky was dark and faded**
> **Solemnly they stated,**
> **"He has to die,**
> **you know he has to die."**

Bali by motorcycle was breathtaking. Narrow roads snaked through lush forests. Waterfalls were plentiful. Dense warm green rainforest air blew through my hair and over my face. Strange jungle sounds surrounded me. Monkeys and other exotic animals, just like you see in the brochures, swung through the trees and scurried across the road. Every so often I would pass through a village too remote to even be on the map. Small brown children with clear eyes and loving smiles would run over to inspect me on my bike. I was the ugly American, Joey Ramone on a rice burner, in search of answers to questions that had not yet been asked, and it felt beautiful.

> **All the children learnin',**
> **from books they were burnin'**
> **Every leaf was turnin',**
> **to watch him die,**
> **you know he had to die.**

By late morning with little gas in my tank I arrived in the tiny coastal town of Candidiasa. I cruised along the main road, the only road, taking note of a few guesthouses and restaurants; in particular a small building painted in traditional reggae colors called The Legend Rock Cafe. I figured that if George were in town that this would certainly be an excellent spot to start looking. I pushed open the door and was immediately engulfed by the smell of strong Indian incense. "Redemption Song" was playing on the juke. Sitting at the bar was a Caucasian woman of about fifty. She was sipping a cup of tea. She looked me up and down. She said, "You're not my guide, are you?"

I shook my head, "No, I don't think so."

She returned to her tea.

I continued, "Actually I just arrived here. I'm looking for a friend of mine. His name is George. Do you know him?"

"I'm sure that I don't," she replied. "I only arrived here a little while ago myself. I'm supposed to meet my guide here. His name is Ketut. You don't look like a Ketut."

"No, my name is Matthew, Matthew Baron. You can call me Matt."

"Nice to meet you Matt. My name is Mildred, Mildred Harrington. You can call me Mildred."

We shook hands. Mildred's story was that she was from Montana, and that her husband Keith had recently died. Against her better judgment, and the expressed opinions of her family members, she had set off on an adventure. She explained how thirty years ago she had been spending time here in Indonesia with her first husband Ron, and their young daughter Sarah, when a freak storm destroyed their boat, costing Ron his life. Miraculously, Mildred and Sarah had survived. At the time, she and Ron were about to uncover what they anticipated would be a huge revelation about the Second Coming of the messiah. After Ron's death, Mildred felt unable to follow through with their research and instead settled down to a more normal life, remarrying and raising a family. Then, soon after her second husband Keith's death, she started having these visions, or hallucinations, persuading her to return to Bali. Finally, when the contact manifested in the form of an angel, she booked her trip. Her guide was to meet her here at the cafe and escort her to Mount Batur. The angel told her that Mount Batur on Bali was exactly where she needed to be.

From behind the bar appeared a native Balinese man with of all things, dreadlocks. In a completely unauthentic Jamaican accent he asked, "Jah brother, can I get you something ta drink?"

I asked, "Do you have any papaya juice? And by any chance do you know a big American guy with a ponytail that goes by the name George?"

He threw some papaya pieces and some

mystery liquid into a small blender. "Sure I know George, mon."

Eagerly I inquired, "Is he here? Is he in town?"

He placed my drink on the bar. "No mon, he left this mornin' on a big sailboat. He and about ten others said they were going ta spend the full moon on one of the Gili islands."

"Shit," I shouted, and I meant it. I chugged my drink, chucked some money on the bar, and said goodbye and good luck to Mildred. I stormed outside and a la DiMaggio kicked the dirt. "Shit, shit, fuck, shit,..... shitfuck!"

Across the rocky road against a background of crystal blue water lie a series of thatched huts scattered among a grove of coconut and papaya trees. Through squinted eyes I glanced up at the glittering blue sun as it ascended higher and higher into the midday yellow sky. The scorching temperature felt like 451 degrees Fahrenheit as it sizzled the top of my head and microwaved my disillusioned soul. Leaving my motorbike behind I trudged to a secluded space of beach and collapsed into the seductive sedative sea. The willing water washed my weary bones and kwikly kooled my karma. I fingered my hair back away from my eyes and tasted the saltiness of the water as it trickled down my face. Off in the distance I spotted a sailboat. Foolishly, I screamed, "George!"

I sat solemnly; silently soaking in the cool sparkling water, watching as the unreachable sailboat slowly disappeared from sight. I decided that for the time being that I needed to forget all about George and instead enjoy a tranquil day in paradise.

I found the manager of the beachfront huts, yet another Ketut, and was soon relaxing in bed under a huge ceiling fan listening to Neil Young's On the Beach. The afternoon heat was oppressive. The music was glorious.

The summer sun
looked down on him,
His mother could
but frown on him,
And all the other sound on him,
He had to die,
you know he had to die.

Several hours later the temperature cooled below 100. With nowhere to go, and no plan of what to do, I decided to take a ride. I dowsed myself with cool clear water at the mundi, pulled on some clothes, and crossed the road to where my bike was parked outside the Legend Rock Cafe. Inside the cafe I could hear "Jammin" playing on the sound system. I followed my thirst, and my instincts, and decided to enter the cafe. Behind the bar was the same Indo-tafarian bartender. He said, "Jah mon, Mildred said you'd be back, and that I was ta give this to ya. She said you could keep it, or return it when the time was right."

He handed me an English/Indonesian dictionary. Inside was a bookmark that opened the book to page three. On the bookmark were the words 'Visualize Whirled Peas'. Highlighted on page three were the Indonesian words anak lakilaki which means son, anak perempuan which means daughter, and terimikasih which means thank you. I slipped the book in my back pocket and ordered a beer. It went down real easy.

I exited the cafe and jumped on my bike. Within seconds I was zooming along the twisting uphill road out of Candidiasa into the hills of southeast Bali. The air kwikly kooled and a few low-lying klouds began to form. Since I was low on gas I decided to head for the next closest town, Tenganan.

A few minutes later I cruised into the

medium size town. Strangely, not a solitary sole was to be found. I sat for a minute with my bike idling, feeling like I had just entered the Indonesian version of *The Twilight Zone*. It just didn't make any sense. Where were all the people? I drove up and down the dirt road through the barren town. Completely dumbfounded I drove on. The winding jungle roads led uphill as the air grew colder still and dark rain clouds gathered overhead. Some monkeys in the road sat eating bananas. The needle on the gas gauge was butting the E. I contemplated heading back to Candidiasa, but decided, "oh fuck it; there must be another town up ahead." I cruised up and over a small embankment, then coasted with the engine off down the other side into the small square at the center of some tiny village. Again everyone was missing. I turned off the ignition and walked up and down the road. Completely puzzled I took out my map of the island. I tried to figure out where I was, but where I was, was nowhere on the map.

I called out, "Ketut!"

Nobody answered. I sat down on my bike feeling confused and seriously spooked. Where did everyone go?

Then, off in the distance, about 100 yards

away, I spotted a single file of people walking up the side of a hill. I started my engine and navigated my way through the tiny maze of streets until I came upon the last few villagers as they exited their simple town temple to join the queue. Finally the very last person, a man just a little older than me, gently closed the temple doors behind him. As he turned to join the line my unexpected presence from the road startled him. He stopped abruptly and accidentally dropped a coconut from his hand. It bounced twice then rolled to my feet. In his other hand he held a machete. He looked down at the coconut, then up into my eyes. He smiled. I silently picked up the coconut and held it out to him. I stood perfectly still as this native man wearing only a sarong slowly approached me. He took his coconut and scampered off to catch up with the end of the line. After about ten paces he paused and looked back at me. Again he smiled. Only this time it was more of a thoughtful, knowing kind of smile, clearly different from the warm calm smile of just a few seconds ago. He waved for me to follow him and join the procession. With the excitement that uncertainty brings I returned his smile and followed the procession up the hill. The rumble of my bike caught the attention of the villagers who seemed to enjoy having me along. As I drove on alongside the line of men and women, young and old, all smiling, encouraging me to join them, I realized that this must be a line of every person that lived in this village. But where could they all be going?

The road ended at a precipice. Below me gentle surf rolled over glistening golden sand. Adjacent to the precipice the unbroken chain of people veered onto a narrow path that immediately disappeared into the dense green jungle. I parked my bike and followed the path around the side of a small hill. It began to drizzle. I looked up at the overcast sky and spotted a majestic temple constructed right into the face of the neighboring hill. As I approached the temple I observed that each villager would remove a flower from the huge floral wreath that adorned the holy structure's entrance. I followed suit by carefully freeing a tiny white blossom which I dropped into my breast pocket as I crossed over into Aoxomoxoa. To my left, many women were preparing a feast. To my right was a large canopied orchestra pit. And straight ahead were eleven steps leading to two open doors. After quickly surveying the grounds I guestimated that in all there must have been about 200 people present. Everyone was dressed in colorful sarongs and barefoot. The light drizzle didn't seem to bother anyone. At the base of the steps, off to one side, a group of men and children gathered. A boy of about 8 approached me and said, "Come see, come see."

So I did.

In the center of the congregation, kneeling, facing each other, were two older men. They were sing-saying some kind of duet, not that much different from 'Hey Joe'. Each man was holding a small bird. The grateful gallery of onlookers occasionally burst into laughter as the two geezers entertained them. Three women stopped to look, shaking their heads in futility at the games that men play. Then off the women went, climbing the mysterious steps and through the open doors. One of the younger men noticed me watching the ascending group of women. He said, "No sarong, no temple."

At once I understood that my casual attire, which did not show the Gods their proper respect, would prevent me from entering the temple's holy grounds.

I turned my attention back to the two old men. They each held their bird up to the sky, which started the children cheering. Then just as I expected them to set the birds free, the men wrenched off the birds' heads with their bare hands and tossed the heads into the jungle. Everyone hugged and cheered as the two men pressed the bleeding bird torsos together. One of the old men looked over at me laughing and whooping. As he peeked into my soul I was overcome by what my high school sweetheart called a 'big and little' feeling. Although difficult to explain exactly, a 'big and little' is when you're aware of your surroundings and happenstances, but at the same time everything around is so completely foreign that you might as well be in a different dimension of existence. And as I stood spellbound in the big and little I couldn't help but think.....here I am on the edge of nowhere, and what could possibly be better for the native's evening ceremony than to sacrifice the new guy.

In what seemed like slow motion, I strolled away from the current situation over to the orchestra canopy where about thirty men were lining up their instruments. There were eight rows of ten metal pots in ascending size order, with the smallest pot the size of a creamer, and the largest as big as a lobster pot. There were four sets of four kettledrums, one in each corner. The rest of the area was filled with rows of congas, bongos and other assorted percussion type instruments. There were also two long rows of woodwinds. In the back of my brain I sensed a Jerry space jam winding down in anticipation of Phil's thunderous bass rumble as "The Faster We Go The Rounder We Get" begins.

A silver haired musician caught my attention and motioned me inside the canopy. He handed me an instrument resembling a recorder and motioned for me to play it. I politely handed him back the instrument and air drummed that I would be more comfortable behind one of four sets of standing conga drums. He gently bit his lower lip and nodded his head several times. Suddenly he was off somewhere in his mind, as though he was having his own big and little. Seconds later when he time-tripped back into reality he looked into my eyes and smiled. He walked toward me placing his hand lightly on my shoulder as he passed. The kindness of his gentle touch broke my own big and little and returned me to moving at normal speed. Where the silver haired musician was in his mind for those few seconds I'll never know. I turned to watch where he was going, but just as he exited the canopy I lost him behind a large group of playing children. My stomach rumbled a tune of its own, and it occurred to me that I was starving.

I headed for where the women had earlier

been preparing the food. I walked over to where an older woman was handing out wooden plate/bowls to some teenage girls. She held out a plate to me, but pulled it back just as I reached for it. She looked me up and down and crinkled up her already crinkled nose at my inappropriate attire. One of the girls said something to her and she again offered me a plate. As I took hold of it she didn't let go. I wrestled back and forth for the plate with the old woman, but let her win as to not cause any conflict. Once again I was plateless, and hungry, and confused. Again the girl said something to the old woman. For the third time she held out a plate. When I hesitated to reach for it she stuck her tongue out at me. Finally the young girl took the plate from the woman and handed it to me.

The girl said, "No sarong, no good. Food there."

I took my plate and thanked the young girl. I walked to where the food was being served and graciously accepted a plateful of unfamiliar cuisine. I sat on the ground across from several families and began sampling the mystery fare. They watched me eat in a friendly curious way, and several of them lightly laughed just as I bit into a rolled up burrito type thing. I chewed three times before my mouth caught fire. As I desperately searched the area for water someone tapped me on the shoulder. It was the teenage girl. She handed me a cup of red beverage, which I happily accepted. I drank the sweet tart liquid, which soothed my scorched mouth and tongue.

She said, "Banas, banas," and waved her hand several times over her slightly open mouth.

Instantly I understood that banas meant hot and repeated back, "Yes, banas, banas."

She smiled and chuckled lightly at my mild discomfort, as did many of the surrounding villagers. I joined in laughing which only made everyone else laugh even more. When the laughing stopped the young girl repeated, "No sarong, no good. You want sarong."

I responded, "Yes, yes I want sarong."

A sarong would allow me to enter the holy grounds and experience the scene inside those two open doors at the top of the steps.

The girl called out, "Ketut."

About ten men looked over, but only the

one she was looking at approached.

She said to me, "My brother Ketut."

Then she said something to him in their native tongue. And he said some stuff back to her. Listening to the two of them converse in their native tongue reminded me of the dictionary that Mildred had given me. I reached into my pocket and opened the book to page three. I committed the three highlighted phrases to memory. Finally the girl said to me, "You go Ketut. Ketut have you sarong."

I responded, "terimikasih."

Ketut and I left the grounds. In silence we made our way through the jungle, back to the road where my bike was parked. Ketut picked up my helmet which was hanging on the handlebars and put it on his head. He grinned ear to ear and somehow reminded me of Danny Devito playing Martini in Cuckoo's nest. I said to him, "I bet a nickel."

Ketut looked at me with a puzzled look. And although he hadn't a clue of what it meant, I couldn't resist adding in my best Nicholson, "This is a dime, Martini. This is shit."

Even though I was extremely low on gas I

hopped on and started the bike. Ketut sat down behind me and off we went, me and Martini, back to the deserted village. Ketut tapped my shoulder and pointed for me to turn down a small dirt road. He squeezed my shoulder, so I stopped. He dismounted the bike and disappeared into a small wooden house. I shut the engine to conserve fuel and got off the bike. I walked down to a brook that ran along a row of similarly built structures. What a totally uncomplicated way of life these people must live. No phones, no lights, no motor cars, not a single luxury. Like Robinson Ca-rusoe, it's primitive as can be.

The cloudy sky was now growing dark. Ketut appeared carrying a beautiful orange and blue sarong. He wrapped the garment around my waist and secured it in a way that to this day I cannot duplicate. I looked down at myself and found humor in the fact that my sarong was not only perfect for this evening, but would also make a great promotional giveaway for Sarong Night at Shea Stadium. I looked over at Ketut who I'm sure had never seen the Mets play and he too was smiling. He still had the helmet on his head. We got back on my bike and headed back to the temple.

Once inside I thanked Ketut and his sister, and made it a point to show off my newly borrowed garment to the old woman with the plates. Again she crinkled her nose in disapproval, then smiled. I returned her smile and made my way to the steps that led to the holy inner sanctum of the temple. At the base of the steps the first native man with the coconut greeted me. He eyed me up and down and approvingly smiled as he admired my sarong. He held out his hand to welcome me to ascend the steps. Excitedly I climbed and upon reaching the top had my first look at what was inside.

Tables overflowing with flowers surrounded a large open courtyard of lush wet grass. About forty men, women, and children were sitting cross-legged scattered in several groups throughout. Directly across on a stage podium several holy men were performing some kind of ritual.

My coconut friend brushed past me and entered the courtyard. I stood watching as he padded over to where several young boys were sitting. I took a deep breath, and with the eyes of the world, or at least the eyes of the village upon me, strode lightly into the courtyard and sat down alone. I curiously watched the holy men as the ritual proceeded, thinking back to the evening just a few months ago when I watched Jerry and the Dead perform in the rain at the Meadowlands. I looked over at 'Captain Coconut' who was explaining something to the boys. One of the boys seemed to be challenging his explanation. He shook his head, took on a look more bemused than exasperated, opened his eyes wide, smiled the same knowing smile I saw earlier, and gave the boy a hug. The other boys then huddled around him in a group hug. In the midst of this beautiful moment he looked my way. A warm feeling of family rushed through me as I called out to him the Indonesian words, "anak lakilaki," and pointed to the boys.

He lightly laughed and releasing the boys called out, "Ketut, Yeoman, Jones."

Three young men along with several other boys appeared and joined his group. My coconut friend pointed to the three young men and said, "anak lakilaki." He then pointed to several of the boys, and motioning to Ketut his first son he repeated, "anak lakilaki." Amazingly, this Indonesian man who was only a few years my senior had three sons and a slew of grandsons. I nodded and smiled. The rain fell harder. I questioningly called out, "anak perempuan?" He smiled and held up four fingers. I opened my eyes wide and we both laughed. The courtyard began to empty as the native people scurried to the perimeter of the grounds to take cover under the tables of flowers as buckets of rain fell from the heavens. Captain Coconut approached me and sat down. The rest of the villagers had by now taken cover so that it was just he and I sitting in what was now a torrential downpour. We looked at each other with water pouring down our faces, laughing hysterically, drowning in the madness of the moment. Even the holy men on the canopied podium had stopped their ritual and were focusing their attention on the two lunatics laughing in the rain.

Eventually the rains returned to a light drizzle. The holy men continued their prayers and people returned to their places. In the distance behind me I heard music playing. I stood up and shared one final magical smile and laugh with Captain Coconut, and made my way out of the holy area.

From atop the steps I peered inside the orchestra pit where the musicians were jamming. As I watched and listened to the mostly percussion orchestra bang and clang, I thought to myself, what a trip! I made my way closer to the music and spotted the silver haired musician as he played his recorder, which was far too soft to hear. He mindfully fingered a few notes then unexplainably looked right at me. He stood up, walked over to me, and took my hand. He led me into the orchestra pit and sat me down directly across from him. He thoughtfully returned to playing his recorder.

The music never stopped. The rain's intensity again increased. Native people squashed themselves into the dry protected pit. Content, I sat in the crammed area with two small children resting their sleeping heads in my lap. Loud rumbling thunder accompanied the band. I looked into the eyes of the silver haired musician. As he gazed back into my eyes he began to slowly squint. And as he did, his face began to morph, until he took on the characteristics of Mickey Hart. The music became quieter and calmer, and in between raindrops and thunderclaps I heard...

Spanish lady come to me
she lays on me this rose
It rainbow spirals
 round and round,
It trembles and explodes
It left a smoking crater
of my mind,
I like to blow away
But the heat came round
and busted me
For smilin' on a cloudy day
Comin', comin', comin' around,
comin' around,
coming around, comin around

The silver haired musician/Mickey Hart rose without effort, took my hand and pulled me to my feet. He led me over to a set of congas where the existing drummer smiled and stepped away. I began to play, and found it easy to join in and keep time to the beat. The silver haired musician walked back to his spot, but instead of picking up his recorder he helped a silver haired woman to her feet. It was the woman who had given me a hard time with the dinner plate. They both looked my way then glided hand in hand through the crowded pit, only to disappear into the rain. As I continued to play my confidence grew and before long I felt as though I was in control. I quickened the pace and accented the beat in certain places,

and all the other musicians followed my lead.
Off in the woods I heard whale noises, which
gave rise to a great reverberating thunder. I
sensed the second verse of The Other One
coming, so I began singing:

> **"Escapin' through the lily fields**
> **I came across an empty space**
> **It trembled then exploded**
> **Left a bus stop in its place**
> **The bus stopped by and I got on**
> **That's when it all began**
> **There was cowboy Neal**
> **At the wheel**
> **Of a bus to never-ever land**
> **Comin', comin', comin' around,**
> **comin' around**
> **Comin' around,**
> **comin' aroww wound"**

The music played the band as the
cacophony of percussion rang through the
sopping hills. The inner sanctum holy men filed
into the center of the orchestra pit then walked
back out. The jam session wound down into
silence as one by one musicians put down their
instruments and followed the big machas back
up the steps and into the holy temple area.

I joined the queue, climbed the steps and
paused at the top. Every villager fell to their

knees as the holy men led the congregation in prayer. I spotted Captain Coconut with his family. He rose and approached me. He took me by the hand and walked me to where his family was all kneeling in prayer. He knelt down and motioned for me to do the same. He offered me a flower and coached me to hold it between my two hands with the petals sticking out on top. As I followed his instruction I realized that because he had given me his prayer flower, he had none. Then I remembered the flower in my breast pocket. I reached in, removed it, and proudly presented it to him. He gratefully took the flower and returned to his praying.

The holy men continued their banter for a few minutes then paused and dispersed throughout the congregation. They collected the offering of flowers from the trancelike villagers and placed them into a large metal bowl. The heavens opened to cleanse us, wash us, and nearly drown us as the rain teemed on. However, this time nobody moved for shelter, and nobody laughed. Again the holy men dispersed, this time with rice in their hands. As one holy man approached, I copied Captain Coconut who had opened his mouth to receive a few grains. I accepted the rice in my mouth, which I chewed and swallowed. The holy man then pressed a few grains of rice against my forehead. The ceremony continued for a few more minutes until someone banged a gong. Everyone stood and cheered and hugged. The rain subsided. People made their way out to the food and music area.

From the entrance to the holy grounds I observed the celebration. Captain Coconut appeared and handed me some red juice. The processional of holy men passed. The oldest of them stopped in front of me and pointed at me. He placed his hands together in a prayer position. I took this as a way to ask me if I had prayed. I put my hands together and nodded in affirmation. He cracked a half smile, squinted, and returned my nod. Then he walked on, gently patting his withered claw of a hand on my shoulder as he passed. His touch ignited my inner essence sending it soaring like an avatar towards the heavens. What a rush!

I finished my juice and sat exhausted on a wet rock, clueless about the time, or the century. My sarong lending friend, Martini, and his sister approached me. I handed back my sarong and gratefully thanked them for their kindness. They smiled in silence as they joined the rest of the village on their way back to their homes.

**And when the day had ended,
with rainbow colors blended
Their minds remained unbended
He had to die,
oh, you know he had to die**

Eventually I made my way back to my motorcycle with the bone dry gas tank. I rolled quietly downhill into the tiny village. Somehow the engine turned over, and I began my journey back to Candidiasa. Running on fumes, and prayers of desperation, the engine mysteriously revved on through the dark drizzling wee hours of morning. Miraculously I guessed correctly at several unfamiliar forks in the road and somehow arrived at what I recognized to be the final hill leading toward the tiny beachfront town. The engine sputtered as my bike choked its way to the peak, only to cease at the very top of the hill. I drew in a deep precipitous breath, feeling the warm moist air tickling my sinuses, and let out a sigh of relief at somehow making it back. Gently I pushed off the wet pavement, starting the bike slowly rolling toward my destination. Suddenly the air dried and cooled, the rain stopped, and the clouds parted, allowing a great bright full moon to light my approach back to my hut near the water. I collapsed onto my bed and passed out.

9 <u>red rocks</u>

Knock, knock, knock. "Mr. Matthew, I bring breakfast now?"

It was Ketut, the manager of the beachfront huts at my door. I groggily answered, "Sure, bring me breakfast."

I splashed some water on my face, and stared at myself in the small mirror hanging on the wall. Water dripped off my stubble-laden cheeks and chin, and glistened over my slightly sunburned nose. Deep inside I felt different, even enlightened by the events of the previous evening. I thought about my lifeless career and mundane life back in New York. A vision of Peggy Lee on the old Ed Sullivan show singing "Is that all there is?" ran across my mind's eye. A knock on the door broke my melancholy trance.

"Mr. Matthew, breakfast on table. I go now."

I exited my hut to find a tray of food on a small table neighboring a wooden chair. On the tray were slices of fresh coconut, pineapple and papaya, a hard-boiled egg with a slice of limp toast, and a cup of hot brown beverage that certainly was not coffee. I filled my belly and sipped at the mostly unsatisfying beverage as a warm breeze blew in off the water. In the distance I heard what I thought was the Dead singing "Not Fade Away". My thoughts turned to my improbable extraterrestrial meeting two nights ago with Buddy, Ritchie and J.P.

All the years combine
they melt into a dream
A broken angel sings
from a guitar
In the end there's just a song
comes crying like the wind
through all the broken dreams
and vanished years

Stella Blue

Not Fade Away transitioned into "Goin' Down the Road", but this wasn't my imagination. My interest piqued, I walked to the next hut. Sitting at a table, eating a duplicate breakfast, listening to a small boom box was a large pony tailed Caucasian. I shook my head to clear the cobwebs before asking, "Are you George?"

"That's me," he answered. "Who are you?"

"My names Matt, Matt Baron." I paused for a second to gather my thoughts. "This probably won't make any sense to you, but I've been trying to find you. You see, I met this girl up in Bangkok named Kylie. She said I might find you on the island Kho Phangan. I traveled through the night to get there, only to find out from some South Africans that you had left for here. But I didn't think I would find you here because just after I arrived, the pseudorasta guy across the street told me you were on a sailboat traveling to some other island."

George sat patiently as I rambled. When I finally came up for air, he asked, "Well, now that you've found me, what do you want?"

Bob Weir screamed the last of the vocals as Goin' Down the Road had changed back to Not Fade Away, which quickly ended with a searing crescendo and a bang.

I continued, "Kylie told me that you had been so distraught over Jerry's death that you felt compelled to uproot and travel. Which is exactly the same thing that I did. And also, because she specifically told me that you had used the phrase, shit sure and ready to tour, which as far as I know is a saying used by my best friend Rich and I, and that's it. I couldn't imagine why anyone else would be saying it."

George took a sip from his mug. He

turned away and spit out the beverage at the base of some plants. The tape hissed, then stopped. He flipped it over and pressed play. "Morning Dew" began. George looked me up and down and lightly chuckled. He said, "shit sure and ready to tour." Again he looked me up and down. He said, "I can solve your mystery with two words."

"Two words," I questioned. "What two words?"

He smiled the smile that I had seen him smile a few nights ago in my dream. He said, "Red Rocks."

"Red Rocks? You mean in Colorado? What about Red Rocks?" No light bulb had flicked on above my puzzled, troubled head.

"Red Rocks, 1978, or was it '79? You were there weren't you," George knowingly inquired?

"Sure, I was there, in '79" I answered. "Go on."

"Let me refresh your memory. It was one hot fucking day. And tickets were really scarce. You were there with your buddy. You didn't have any tickets, but you kept on saying that somehow you would get in, that you always figured out some way to get in."

"That's right, my best friend Rich and I were on tour, summer of '79. Like lots of people that day, we didn't have tickets and 'needed a miracle'. We arrived at Red Rocks hours before the Dead would begin, hopeful of scoring tickets, or, as we had heard was possible, sneaking in, by climbing the massive red rocks that encompass the amphitheater, with hopes of finding some hidden pass that would bring us inside. Since nobody had extra tickets, and nearly everyone was trying to cop one, Rich and I took a shot at climbing in. After several futile attempts, and one close call with a park ranger, we decided to call it quits. We found salvation at the base of the rocks under a makeshift wooden shelter that housed a water fountain and a few wooden benches."

"That's right." George knowingly encouraged me. "What was the scene at the shelter?"

"People came and went. Some guy with a guitar sang "Cream Puff War", "Squeeze Box", "Dead Flowers" and others. Joints, bowls, bongs and even a four hose glass hookah filled the air and our lungs with samples of green, gold, red, and brown. There was even some guy there doling out spoons of blow from a seemingly endless supply of little brown vials. He was there with these two blonde hotties that were dancing and spinning, even though the show wouldn't begin for another few hours."

George interrupted, "That was me with the endless vials and the two blonde hotties. And you and your friend were two kids from New York that had never tried cocaine, and wound up snorting enough to keep your spines tingling and your eyes sparkling for days. You were wearing t-shirts that on the front read, 'Blow out our speakers just one more time', and on the back, 'Shit sure and ready to tour'. I've been saying it ever since."

I immediately recalled the t-shirts that Rich and I had made for our trip cross-country that summer of '79. Since it had worn out some fifteen years ago, it never crossed my mind as a clue to solving why George would be saying shit sure and ready to tour.

Enlightened, I responded, "I see said the blind man. And who were the two spinning girls?"

"The two girls were Jennifer and her younger sister Valerie. The three of us were sharing a flat in Iowa City. Jen and I were earning degrees at Grinnell College, and Valerie was finishing her senior year of high school, and working at a record store. Just after Valerie's graduation we loaded up my dad's old '51 woodie and went on tour following the Dead. Oh what a splendid summer it was!"

"Whatever happened to Jennifer and Valerie?" I asked.

"I married Jennifer the following summer, and settled in San Francisco. And Valerie is now living in New York City."

I couldn't believe my ears. I blurted, "Is she married?"

Straight away I realized the absurdity of my question, but like a fall leaf floating freely toward Earth, or perhaps more like a watermelon being dropped from a helicopter onto concrete, the question straightforwardly spilled from my mouth.

George shot me an appropriately bewildered look. Before he could answer, the door to his hut opened and out stepped a beautiful blonde woman dressed in a sarong and bikini top.

"Morning Georgie," she said as she leaned

over and gave him a kiss.

"Morning my sweet, this is Matt."

She turned and looked at me. She smiled a lazy smile and spun off the deck onto the grass. Silver bangles on her ankles emitted a slight jingle. She blew George another kiss and started toward the beach. In the shade of a palm tree she sat and began to meditate.

George broke the silence. "That lovely creature is my wife, Jennifer. But as I recall you were inquiring about her sister, Valerie. As far as I know, she's available."

"Maybe when I get back to New York I could meet up with her?"

"Why wait, she'll be here in Candidiasa later this afternoon."

"Later this afternoon," I incredulously questioned. Where is she?"

"Out sailing on my friend Barry's yacht. Yesterday morning we all set out for the tiny Gili Islands, just off the coast of Lombok. The plan was to spend full moon on this quaint little island, Gili Trawangan, but when we arrived we were met by some hostile Indonesian military officials who were not allowing anyone onto the island. Apparently the Indonesian government had sold the island and several other small nearby islands to one of the large Hotel chains. The military were there evicting the indigenous island people from their homes and businesses, as they had no official claim to the property. Barry, the owner and captain of our ship decided it would be best to altogether avoid the situation. Instead we held our own private full moon celebration onboard, then in the wee hours he dropped Jen and I back here to get some sleep. Valerie and the others spent the night sleeping under the stars, anchored somewhere off the coast. They're due back later today. You could join us all for dinner tonight. You could meet Valerie then."

"Sure, thanks, that sounds great."

My good fortune of finding George, just as I had given up looking, and my even greater fortune of having imminent plans to meet and have dinner with the spinning sirens of my recent pipe dreams, seemed like more of a cosmic aligning of fate than just some wild coincidence. New York, my job, and Alexandra seemed light years away. I felt one with nature. But was I crazy for doing and thinking all that I had done and thought, or was it just my imagination, running away with me? George summoned me back to the here and now.

"And by the way,....... did you get in at Red Rocks?"

"Yeah, we got in, we always got in. After a full day of partying, with no tickets to be had, Rich and I were actually ready to give up and pack it in. We started walking down that long dusty red road that led to the parking lot when we came across two girls who were hitting on a joint as they hurried back toward the venue entrance. With the show about to begin the girls each took a final hit then handed me the roach. As we completed the pass I noticed a stamp on the back of the girl's hand. It was a double RR, in dark red, about one inch high. The girl explained that she and her friend had already been inside, and that their hands were stamped in order to re-enter the amphitheater. Remarkably, one of the girls had an eyebrow pencil, which enabled me to do a fair job of duplicating the stamp onto our hands. When the girls hurried inside, flashing their stamped hands to the guards, Rich and I followed suit, and waltzed in without so much as a hitch."

Then it hit me like a ton of bricks. "Then you were there when that guy fell to his death?"

George's head dropped. He nodded yes. He somberly said, "Yup, I watched him fall." He paused, then looked directly into my eyes. "Did you see him?"

I felt the feeling of cold electricity run between us. I swallowed hard and nodded. I too had witnessed the tragic fall.

While we were partying under the wooden shelter, I spotted a lone climber about 200 yards away who seemed to be struggling. He had climbed onto a moderately steep grade that also sloped away from the safety of the nearby rocks. Every time he tried to inch down the grade, gravity would draw him closer to the edge of doom. He struggled for some five or ten minutes until he slid off the sloping rock, and free fell some forty to fifty feet. His landing blocked by numerous huge boulders. I immediately ran to find a park ranger, and within minutes found one. I explained to the ranger what I had seen. I thought about how earlier, Rich and I had stupidly been climbing on those same rocks, and how it might have been one of us taking that terrible fall. I hoped that the poor fellow had somehow miraculously survived.

He didn't.

**When all the cards are down
there's nothing left to see
There's just the pavement left
and broken dreams
In the end
there's still that song
comes crying like the wind
down every lonely street
there's ever been**

Stella Blue

"Where were you when Jerry died," I asked?

George said, "I was on business in the Hamptons in New York. I was having lunch at this really cool luncheonette in some tiny town called Eastport, where all the milkshakes are named for different blues and rock guitarists. I'm sitting at the counter when the owner, this guy they call 'Homefries' enters the luncheonette and announces to the patrons and staff that he just heard over his car radio that Jerry Garcia of the Grateful Dead had died? I blurted out, "What?"

He repeated that Jerry had been found earlier that day, dead in his bed at the rehab center where he was receiving treatment. My heart slid into my shoes. I held onto the counter with both hands and stared blankly into my Jimi Hendrix shake. I thought to myself, 'Jerry... dead, no way, he just can't be dead.' It was like I had lost a brother. Homefries stopped the Peter Green/Fleetwood Mac disc that was playing, and replaced it with *American Beauty*. We listened in silence to "Ripple". I got teary eyed when Jerry sang, 'Let there be songs, to fill the air'. Numbly I drove up island to catch The Allman Brothers that night at Jones Beach."

"No way," I responded in disbelief. "I was at that same Allman's show. The night Jerry died. With that eerie pinkish red sky before the show started. I ducked out of work early that day, and picked up my buddy Moose, and off we headed for the concert. When we arrived we got the sad news. We smoked a joint in the parking lot, and reminisced about how Jerry had played this "Sugaree" or that "Bertha". The whole night everyone was dumbstruck and subdued, and that sky was totally eerie."

"Yeah," George concurred, "that red eerie sky. I saw a sky like that only one other time in my life, up on a little mountain in New Zealand called Takaka. Red, red pink eerie sky, hell if I know why...... Anyway, a few days later when my business trip to New York was over I flew back to my life in San Francisco. Only while waiting at the baggage claim I impulsively purchased a ticket and flew to Fiji. That's where I hooked up with Barry, my buddy with the yacht. Jennifer met up with me later on, on Tasmania, and a few weeks later Valerie flew out and met us here on Bali. That's when I met Kylie from Australia. She was in Candidiasa to meet with some friends of hers from back home. Since her friends weren't due until evening, she wound up spending the day with Jen and me. Where did you say you met her?"

"In Bangkok, on Khao San Road. I had just arrived from New York. When I told her that it sounded as though she was on tour, you came up. She told me that I might find you at the full moon party on Kho Phangan. But when I got there, those people from South Africa told me that you were headed here."

"Ah yes," suddenly George was impersonating W.C. Fields, " the South African contingent at the full moon party on Kho Phangan, I participated in a game of chance with several of the local natives during the Ping-Pong finals held at the highpoint of the rainy season, many people fell ill due to swimmer's ear."

I applauded George's effort. In my best Groucho I added, "So what are your plans, that is after they tear you down and put up a movie theatre where you're sitting?"

George returned the applause.

"Well the first thing I'm gonna do is make some real coffee, because this brown bear piss tastes like brown moose piss. How about a cup of freshly ground Kona?"

**I've stayed in every
blue-light cheap hotel
Can't win for trying
Dust off those rusty strings just
one more time
Gonna make em shine**

"Kona, no way, I'd give my left nut for a cup of Kona right now."

George chuckled, "You can keep your nut."

He lit the Bunsen burner at his feet and poured some bottled water into a metal pot. From a green Jansport he removed a Pyrex coffee press and a sturdy candy tin with the word Kona written on a piece of tape on top. He twisted open the tin, which let out a gentle phffft as the vacuum released. Inside the tin were beautiful fresh coffee beans, which George poured into a battery operated hand held coffee grinder. Brrwhirrr, brrwhirrr, brrrwhirrr, George offered me a whiff of the ground coffee. It smelled wonderful.

George continued, "I'll probably hang out here for a few more days, and then Jen and I are off to the Philippines for a few weeks. My father was stationed there during World War II. I've always wanted to check it out. Then it's back to Stanford to teach Calculus."

"Calculus, no way."

"That's right," George poured the boiling water into the press and produced two mugs from his pack. One had a red dancing bear on it, and written on the other was Davis Chiropractic, Catch the Spiz. He pressed the coffee, then poured it into the two mugs. He handed me the mug that said Catch the Spiz and said, "What about you? What do you do when you're not chasing strangers about the planet?"

"Well up until a few days ago I was gainfully employed by the Manhattan law firm of Goldberg, Greenberg, Trachtenberg, Ditkoff, Kowalicek, Brannigan, Spilatti and DeNunzio. I'm supposed to be marrying some society girl. Back in New York I'm probably about as normal a guy as you could find. Now I'm just a hippie lost in a sea of Winnebago's."

"What does that mean?" Asked George.

I sipped at the piping hot coffee. "I'm not quite sure. It was written on the bathroom wall at a truck stop just outside West Stockbridge, Massachusetts. Rich and I had stopped there on our way to our first Dead show, at Englishtown."

"Well maybe it means that although you're comfortable in your skin and your surroundings, you're uncertain of where you are, where you are headed, or where you would like to be headed. Does that make any sense?"

**It all rolls into one
and nothing comes for free
There's nothing you can hold
for very long
And when you hear that song
come crying like the wind
it seems like all this life
was just a dream**

Stella Blue

I pondered what George had said. Segments from the previous evening flashed through my mind; laughing with Captain Coconut in the pouring rain, Mickey Hart and the ornery old woman walking hand in hand, the touch of the ancient sage, and the children resting their pure, content, completely trusting heads in my lap as they slept. I knew, right then, that I would never marry Alexandra when I returned, or perhaps, crazy, if I returned.

I caught myself deep in thought, scratching the top of my head with both hands. I sheepishly turned to George. He was paying me no mind, peering out to sea through a pair of binoculars.

"Don't think so hard, you're gonna hurt your head," George chuckled.

I sighed. "Sometimes life can be so overwhelming,... and the past few days have been a mountain." I realized that a few days ago I would never have said something as vague as 'been a mountain'. "So George," I asked, feeling like Danielsahn asking Mr. Miyagi for the secret in *The Karate Kid*, "where can I find the answers?"

George shrugged his shoulders, "Hell if I know." He paused. "If you get confused, listen to the music play." He reached into his pocket and pulled out a fatty. "What say we have a smoke, finish our coffee, and go do some snorkeling?" He grinned, lit the joint, and added, "You did say Kona was your blend, didn't you?"

10 dengue

Very stoned, George and I strolled down to the water where we were met by a teenage boy named Ketut driving an extremely narrow, extremely shallow, canoe-like hollowed out log, propelled by a tiny outboard motor. I thought to myself about the time with Rich when I had tipped our canoe on a lake somewhere up in Nova Scotia, Canada. The water stung like a million tiny icicles as we swam to shore towing the canoe. Rich called me a jerk for days. To this day I don't know what made me lean over and roll that canoe. Perhaps it had been the mushrooms.

"Rainbow Reef Mr. George?" Asked Ketut as we settled into the motorized potato chip vessel.

"Yes Ketut, Rainbow Reef, terimikasih."

George leaned way back, took in a deep breath and stretched out his arms, balancing like a glider as we buzzed out to sea. I sat in the middle, dead center, wary of tipping. Off in the distance, over George's right shoulder, I caught sight of a jagged monolith sticking some twenty or thirty feet straight up out of the sea.

"Rainbow Reef," George said to the sky. Then he turned his gaze down toward me, "I don't know if Jerry ever dove in these waters, but when I'm down there, with all the fish and the coral and the quiet peaceful vibe, I sense that if he were along, he'd be digging it.

The mild chop of our craft over the water was slowly and gently turning my insides green, and the scorching sun on the top of my head burned like a hot iron. I took a swig from my water bottle, but found that I wasn't all that thirsty. Actually, I was really starting to feel like crap, but I was also looking forward to snorkeling, and eagerly anticipating meeting Valerie for dinner that evening. I forced myself to take another swallow of water. I hoped that I'd feel better once I got into the water.

George tossed me a pair of flippers and goggles. I carefully rolled off the boat and into the water, being extra careful not to tip, and pulled on my gear. The clear blue water felt cool, but somehow my body and especially my head were ablaze. I followed George as we lazily swam toward Rainbow Reef. All kinds of colorful fish surrounded me, paying me no mind as they went about their daily fish business. The undersea portion of the reef was teeming with creatures too bizarre to tell if they were plants or animals. Everything ebbed and flowed along with the gentle tide, like a scene out of *Yellow Submarine*. George submerged himself about five feet, unclipped a knife from his belt and delicately pried a few spiny sea urchins from the reef. Carefully he snared the aquatic porcupines in a mesh bag that was tied to his ankle. I floated on the surface breathing through my rubber tube, surveying this strange and wonderful underwater world. After a few minutes we both paused with our heads just above the water's surface. I removed the snorkel from my mouth.

"What are you going to do with those things in the bag?"

"Eat them, of course. Haven't you ever had uni?"

"Sure, lots of times, but it didn't look anything like that."

"You'll see."

"Why do you call it Rainbow Reef?"

"Can you dive?"

"Sure, as long as we don't go too deep."

"Then take a deep breath and follow me."

George removed his mask and spit into it, rinsed it, and fit it snugly over his face. Then he went under. I followed his example and soon joined him about ten feet below the surface. He waved for me to follow him into an opening in the reef. Already my head was signaling my lungs to breathe, but I followed him anyway. Within the reef was a cavern. On one side was a huge band of multicolored neon arches, more beautiful than anything I had ever seen. I was mesmerized. I looked over at George, smiled, then bolted. It took forever to reach the surface. I drew in air like a newborn.

Back on shore, George shook five black spiny sea urchins from his bag, snatched up one of the creatures by a single pointy spine and cautiously flipped it over, resting it atop an Igloo cooler next to his hut. Hidden amongst all the spines was a tender circular sucker which George carefully placed his knife against. With all the danger safely cast aside, George, with one good push, split open the sea urchin. Inside, in the design of a spoke, lie five pinky size orange strips of uni filet. George gently freed the briny morsels and placed them onto a ceramic dish. I sat watching through exhausted stoney eyes as George shucked the remaining sea urchins. Just as he completed his task a freshly bathed Jennifer appeared from around the hut.

"Hello darling." Jennifer smootched George atop his head. "I thought I heard something back here."

"Your sashimi order has just arrived." George offered Jennifer the dish of raw uni.

Jennifer snarfed down a piece. She closed her eyes and hummed a yummy noise as she rolled the slimy delicacy around in her mouth. George observed his wife's delight, grinning like a madman.

Jennifer quickly regained herself. "I'm off to meet the boat. Barry said they'd be coming in about now." She turned to me and said, "I'll tell Valerie that she has a dinner date for this evening. I'm sure she'll be excited." She paused and scrutinized me for a second. "Are you feeling all right Matt? You look a little tattered."

I lied. "Sure, I'm fine. Just a bit worn out by the smoke and the snorkeling."

George fed Jennifer another piece of uni.

"Mmmmmmmmm...," she shut her eyes and hollowed in her cheeks as she enjoyed the delectable treat. Knowingly and lovingly she surveyed the wide grinning George and said,

"You, you, I know what you're up to." She kissed George flush on his mouth. Then placing her arm against his chest to keep some distance, she said in a fairly authentic English accent, "No time for the old in-out love, I just came to read the meter." She spun off on her way.

George followed her shapely tush as she headed toward the shore. He turned to me and said, "Fresh uni is a powerful aphrodisiac. It can bring a woman's blood to boil and turn a man into a jackhammer. Here, try a piece."

He held up a sliver of the slimy orange gooze.

I fainted.

Behind blue eyes my body temperature soared until molten lava flowed through my veins. All ran red as my insides burst into flames, igniting like the human torch from the Fantastic Four. The world around me vanished, and banas... banas...I was frying, deep frying, my new world an all-consuming fireball that ravaged me from head to toe. Could I be dead; my years spent as an opportunistic yang attorney tipping the scales of my mostly righteous yin behavior in favor of an eternity spent burning in hell?

Suddenly, I became aware of being carried, but like a piece of raw uni I was limp and lifeless. I was placed onto a bed, where I lay still as a statue, totally drained, the neon brilliance of rainbow reef flickering through my brain, until even thinking produced weakness and pain. Sometime later I sensed foreign hands on my forehead, and from a faraway place perceived voices around me saying, "He's burning up." Then the hands lightly rubbed my neck and crunching sounds reverberated deep inside my head as my neck was turned this way and that. Tidal waves of absolute energy raced down my spine, connecting my fading spirit with something greater. More time passed. I dreamed of beautiful spinning blondes, swirling golden leaves, and the Dead playing "Sugar Magnolia".

I awoke briefly, aware of a cool compress on my head. I felt like a train had hit me. I tried to sit up, but could barely raise my shoulders off the pillow. Through glassy eyes I recognized what appeared to be an angel, in white, sitting in a chair next to my bed. I tried to speak, but could only manage a cough. My throat felt like sandpaper. The angel supported my head and fed me some water. I took a few sips and rested my head down on the pillow. I felt weak and horrible, but at least with an angel beside me I figured I couldn't be in hell.

I drifted off into another dream. This time I was standing at the altar, waiting to get hitched. Alexandra was standing beside me wearing a brown dress and holding a leash with a diamond studded collar. I was supposed to say 'I do', but all I could manage was a weak dry cough. Then the angel in white descended from the ceiling and Alexandra vanished. The angel took my hand and I awoke.

Sitting beside me, holding my hand, was a blonde haired woman in white. She offered me a drink of water, which I thankfully accepted. She removed the compress from my head and placed her hand on my forehead and said, "I think your fever has finally broken."

Not yet fully back, I opened my bleary eyes and asked, "Who are you?"

"I'm Valerie, Jennifer's sister."

I was dazed and confused. Snippet visions of the whirlwind past week sped through my tired, confused mind. I struggled to focus my eyes.

The sweet voice continued, "You blew me off for dinner a few nights ago, but I remember you from back at Red Rocks and thought you might need a little TLC, seeing how you've been unconscious for most of the last three days."

Outside it was night. "Have I been sick?"

"Dengue fever, real bad. Lucky for you Dr. Barry was here. He adjusted you, and gave me instructions about what to do and what to watch for. For a while we weren't sure if you were going to pull through."

I mumbled, "It must have been the curse."

"I don't know about any curse." She gently stroked my forehead and smiled. "But it sure is a relief that you're going to be fine."

I wasn't dead, or in heaven, or hell, but I was most certainly in the company of an angel. I closed my eyes and drifted off to sleep. I dreamed I was driving my BMW convertible on the twisting roads through the hills of Bali. A motorcycle pulled alongside. It was Jerry. He passed me, so I followed. Now we were driving on the Hana Highway on Maui. Jerry pulled off by the seven sacred pools. I followed him by foot along a trail that passed beneath a waterfall. When we came out on the other side, we were standing on the moon, with red moon dust and mushrooms growing at our feet.

I said, "Jerry, ever since you died, I don't know if I'm coming or going. My world was so much more settled when you were in it. Now I'm not even sure of who I am."

Suddenly Jerry was holding a banjo. He began picking. He sang, "Nothing you can do, but you can learn how to be you in time. It's easy." He turned his back to me, and lightly kicked up some moon dust as he headed off toward the mountains of the moon. I watched Jerry lunar bounce along the shadowy landscape until he disappeared into the void. I looked at the Earth in the distance, admiring its beauty and magnitude. My dream mind connected with my conscious mind to trigger my memory to recall when I awoke that the choices we make in life are reflections of who we are, and all we may become. For we all possess the potential to make immense contributions, so long as we recognize, all you need is love.

I knew right then as I dreamed, that I had to let go of Jerry, and this was okay.

11 <u>encore</u>

I awoke alone in my hut, feeling weak, but hungry. I pushed open the wooden shades at my window just as the sun, a raspberry fireball, began climbing the horizon. Slowly, I got up out of bed and shuffled gingerly outside to greet the new day. The wet morning dew on the short green turf felt wonderfully cool on the soles of my feet. I headed for the shore, plopped myself down on the sand and stared out to sea. I took a deep breath and hocked up some crud. In solitude I reflected.

'Life can be such a trip. Like when you fly half way around the world on a whim, in search of something you hope will fill the emptiness in your life, track down the quixotic, not there fragment of an absurd, obscure perquacky, catch the dengue curse and nearly barbeque to death, awaken next to the girl of your dreams, my dreams, my pipe dreams, a spinning angel that I've been subconsciously longing to meet for the past sixteen years, who days ago didn't exist in my world, and not only is she available, but she is happy to see me. Yeah, life's some crazy shit.'

Simultaneously two great whales a few hundred yards away rose from the depths toward the sky and fell back into the sea causing a massive double splash. And in the blink of an eye they were gone, as though their presence had been only a dream.

"How truly beautiful," I heard Valerie utter from behind me, her soothing tone blending in seamlessly with the majestic event that had just occurred.

Fully in tune with the moment, I was not at all startled. In fact, I slowly looked over my shoulder and softly replied, "Hi."

Valerie sat down next to me and looked out to sea. Impulsively I took her hand and we looked into each other's eyes. Silence. We both laughed. Again we both looked out to sea. Again we looked into each other's eyes. Her hand still in mine. My stomach let out a huge rumble.

"You must be starving."

I nodded yes. Strangely, intuitively, I knew she was thinking about how sick I had been. In her eyes I saw genuine concern, yet she didn't really know anything about me. She smiled and took my other hand. We pulled each other up.

"C'mon," she led me back toward the huts.

"I'll make us some breakfast."

Hand in hand we walked to her hut. I sat on the edge of her bed as she lit the burners on her propane stove and poured some water into some pots.

"Thank you for taking care of me when I was sick."

"You're welcome." She smiled. "Actually it was Dr. Barry who took care of you. I just sat with you a lot, and watched to make sure that you didn't stop breathing. George and Jennifer sat with you too. You had us really worried.

"Who is Dr. Barry?"

"Dr. Barry is a chiropractor that George knows. He doesn't practice full time anymore. He spends most of his time sailing his yacht around the world. He's a childhood friend of George's. He adjusted your neck last night when your temperature was going through the roof. Then he told me you'd be thirsty and that your fever would break. And that's what happened."

"Well it sure is good to be back. For a while I felt like I actually might be dying, but then I looked over and saw this angel watching over me and I knew I'd be all right. As it turns out, you were that angel."

Valerie curtsied, then returned to tending to our breakfast. "Believe me, I'm no angel."

She cutely wrinkled her nose, which reminded me of the old woman with the plates on the mountain, then handed me a cup of black coffee and a bowl of oatmeal with raisins. Instantly I time tripped back to my kitchen in New York City, on the morning that I had booked my flight to Bangkok. Surreptitiously I searched the floor of the hut for broken eggs, but found none. I tasted the oatmeal. It was delicious.

We ate in silence, comfortable silence. I felt exhilarated as the hot coffee and carbohydrates raced from my stomach into my bloodstream providing me with my first nourishment and caffeine in days. Or was the exhilaration from being close to Valerie?

"Good?" Valerie smiled and chuckled to herself. I had devoured my oatmeal and inhaled my coffee.

"Yes, it was delicious. Thank you"

She poured me more coffee. "Do you

believe in fate?" Valerie dropped a watermelon of her own.

"Well, sure, I mean, I guess so. Why?"

"The night of the last full moon I was on Dr. Barry's boat anchored off the coast. Everyone on the boat was partying, but I felt a strange uneasiness that propelled me to quietly slip away and sit alone. Off in the distance, up in the hills just outside Candidiasa, amidst the clear peaceful night, I spotted this tiny isolated storm, a real boomer. Anyway, I'm sitting under this huge full moon watching this full on storm when all of a sudden I'm caught in the Phil Zone. And suddenly I'm thinking about the Dead playing "The Other One" at a show I attended in Denver, at McNichols Arena with Jen and George back in the late seventies. Then for no reason I can explain, I'm thinking about this kid that I interacted with briefly the day before the McNichol's show, at Red Rocks."

She paused to take a sip of coffee. I sat quietly, giving her my full attention, mesmerized by her easy way and classic good looks, blown away because she was describing how she had been observing from a distance my full moon experience of a few nights ago.

Valerie continued, "I had been partying all

day long with Jen and George on the grounds at Red Rocks, and I'm watching myself spin, and I'm going around and around, and every time I go around I notice this young guy watching me. And I remember how George was impressed with this guy and his friend, and he invites them to join our party. And when they join I remember thinking how this guy was kind of cute and shy and stoned and funny, someone that I'd like to know, only the show was starting soon and once we went inside I never saw him again. So that's what I mean when I asked if you believe in fate. I find myself thinking about you, after all these years for no apparent reason, and the next day Jennifer tells me you're in Candidiasa waiting to meet me for dinner.

I walked over to Valerie and kissed her on her soft, full mouth. Surprised, she froze for a second, then melted into my arms.

I said, "I'm sorry, I'm not sure why I did that."

She looked deeply into my eyes and replied, "There must be ways to find out, love is the way they say that's really struttin' out." She tenderly kissed me back. She tasted like spring.

12 goodbye jerry

Wednesday evening I arrived back in New York. I had been gone for just over a week. I phoned Alexandra to tell her the wedding was off, but she saved me the trouble by being in Paris with another guy. What had happened was, when I turned up a complete no show the previous Friday night, Alexandra flew with her mother and her aunt to a spa in Arizona. While there, she met the very eligible bachelor, Rob Copper, the Hollywood actor from the television hit, *The Adventures of Dick Deluxe*, and he had invited her along. Thanks Rob.

If my words did glow
with the gold of sunshine
And my tunes were played
on the harp unstrung
Would you hear my voice
come through the music?
Would you hold it near
as it were your own?

Thursday morning I returned to work. Lisa had covered for me magnificently, clarifying to my bosses my acute distress over a close friend's death. 'The Rajah' extended his sympathies, and immediately insisted that I extend my leave by relaxing through the weekend at his friend Blake Monroe's swanky

Easthampton estate. Since Valerie wouldn't be back in New York until the following Wednesday, I decided to soiree' in the Hamptons. However, the weekend's relaxation was short-lived, as two mobsters turned up dead in Sagaponack Bay the morning following Monroe's Friday Evening party. Welcome back to reality.

It's a hand-me-down,
the thoughts are broken
Perhaps they're better
left unsung
I don't know, don't really care
Let there be songs to fill the air

When I popped through the front door of my parent's house on Thursday afternoon my mother hugged me and cried. I said, "C'mon mom I've only been away a week. I spent months away at summer camp, and besides, I'm 35 years old."

Holding me tightly, Mom looked into my eyes and said, "You've been away for much longer than a week. And it's my job to worry."

Of course Mom was right, but now I was back. And I knew it.

My father hardly knew I was gone. And as

I explained to my parents how Valerie and I had magically found each other on Bali, he sat silently in his recliner, switching between TV channels. When I said that things were over with Alexandra he set down his remote and said, "Smart boy, like I tried to tell you, you shouldn't marry for money. You can always borrow it for less."

Ripple in still water
When there is no pebble tossed
Nor wind to blow

That evening I met up with Rich at Pete's Tavern to tell him about my adventure, and, of course, about Valerie. When I arrived he was already at the bar, enjoying a black and tan, explaining to a couple of model wannabes how he had connections with Elite. He gave the brats free passes to a nightclub called Webster Hall and told them he would be in the main floor bar with the pool tables later tonight after one. Then he told them he had some important business to discuss with me regarding the new Johnny Depp film and sent them on their way. He ordered me the same as his and said, "Evening slick, so..... I hear you've given the ball and chain her unconditional release, and decided to waive the player to be named later to trade up for a blast from the past."

We firmly shook hands as I responded, "That's right, pig boy. Wait 'til I give you the lowdown. And about your recently departed companions, didn't you ever see *Raging Bull*? I don't think either of those girls was a day over fourteen."

The bartender set my beer on the bar. I raised my glass and said, "Here's to spinning blondes and angels in white."

Rich clinked his glass against mine and added, "Yeah, and to the Stray Cat Blues."

We both took manly swallows.

I said, "Alexandra's off in Paris with some Hollywood B actor, and it looks like I'm off the hook."

Rich nodded, "Well just as well, and since you're not going to marry her, I might as well tell you, I always thought she was a nimrod." He punctuated the word nimrod by ricocheting a powerful fart off the front of the bar.

We ate bloody steaks and talked and laughed and drank. When I explained about how fate had brought Valerie and I together, all Rich could say was, "Amazing, amazing, amazing, AMAZING!"

**Reach out your hand
if your cup be empty
If your cup is full
may it be again
Let it be known
there is a fountain
That was not made
by the hands of men**

A few days later Valerie returned to the city. Instantly my life in New York took on new meaning. Her apartment in Soho was just a quick eleven minute walk away through Washington Square Park. I cut back on my hours with the firm and spent quality time with her, always laughing, sharing, and loving. We caught two of the Allman Brothers shows at the Beacon, and checked out Phish and Widespread Panic. We had great seats for the Other Ones and of course felt right at home with the Dead crowd, but when the music started I felt as though there was a gaping hole in it. It was like a shiny new Jaguar ready to be driven down the highway, except that the steering wheel was missing.

There is a road,
no simple highway
Between the dawn
and the dark of night
And if you go
no one may follow
That path is for
your steps alone

I think of Jerry often. He wasn't handsome, but the kindness of his face was a lovelight. And in an age of physical fitness, he was neither physical nor fit. However, the enormity of his power became instantly evident as soon as he strapped on his Fender. He was a user and abuser of illegal substances, however this only added to his vulnerability and mystique as Captain Trips, the unassuming leader of a passive rebellion against the Leave it to Beaver mindset of critical, oft afraid, narrow minded, stuck in their stuff, piss in your cheerios, conservative John Wayne wannabees.

Ripple in still water
When there is no pebble tossed
Nor wind to blow

From humble beginnings and a somewhat troubled upbringing, Jerry went on to influence an entire generation of misfits, professionals, and everyone in between with enough curiosity to get on the bus and come along for the ride.

He was about love. He was about peace. He was about freedom. He was about brotherhood. He was about opening minds. But mostly he was about music, beautiful music.

He was the ultimate hippie personification of the American dream. He was Jerome John Garcia. Man, how I miss him.

**You who choose
to lead must follow
But if you fall you fall alone
If you should stand
then who's to guide you?
If I knew the way
I would take you home**

Goodbye Jerry.

About The Author

Fall Without Jerry
is the first novel written
by Henri Rosenblum.

It arose
from the emptiness he experienced
when he realized
there would be no more Grateful Dead
concerts.

An ex-college professor, world traveler,
and veteran of over sixty Dead shows,
Henri presently resides on Long Island in NY
where he practices chiropractic and nutrition
and directs POWER ON Wellness Center.

Anyone who wishes to share thoughts
about what they felt when Jerry died,
thoughts on being kind,
or a review of Fall Without Jerry
can do so at **www.Deadventures.com**.

In Nocte Consilium
Zzzzzzzzzzzzzzzz

Proof

Made in the USA
Charleston, SC
04 March 2015